DON'T LOOK
BEHIND YOU

LOIS DUNCAN

DON'T LOOK BEHIND YOU

Delacorte Press

Published by
Delacorte Press
Bantam Doubleday Dell Publishing Group, Inc.
666 Fifth Avenue
New York, New York 10103

Library of Congress Cataloging in Publication Data

Duncan, Lois, 1934–
    Don't look behind you / by Lois Duncan.
        p.   cm.
    Summary: Seventeen-year-old April finds her comfortable
life changed forever when death threats to her father, a witness
in a federal case, force her family to go into hiding under assumed
names and flee the pursuit of a hired killer.
    ISBN 0-385-29739-4
    [1. Mystery and detective stories.]   I. Title.
PZ7.D9117Dm   1989
[Fic]—dc19   88-30045
                                                              CIP
                                                              AC

Manufactured in the United States of America
June 1989
10 9 8 7 6 5 4

BG

For Jim and Mary Lavin,
Betsy, Jamie and Michael,
and, of course,
Clare

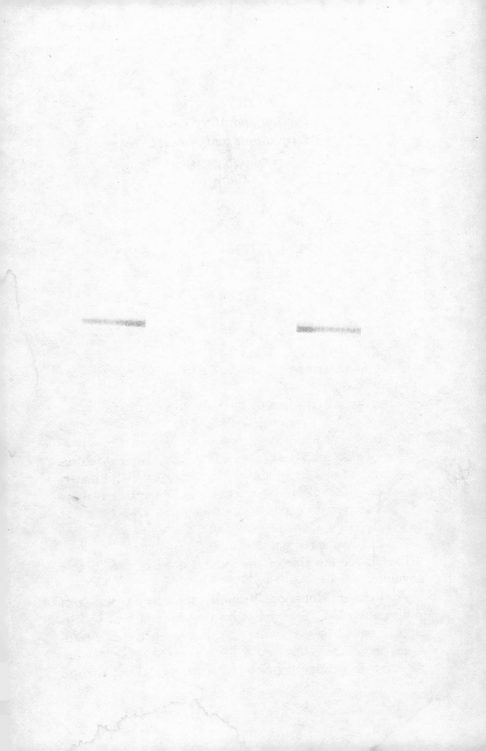

1

The world as we knew it ended for us on a Tuesday afternoon in May.

There were four of us in the family, if you didn't count Lorelei. Our last name was Corrigan. My father worked for an airline called Southern Skyways, and my mother was an author of children's books. My little brother Bram—George Bramwell, Jr.—was a third grader at Crestwood Elementary School. His claim to fame was that he had one blue eye and one brown one. My name was April, and I was an eleventh grader at Springside Academy. My claim to fame was that I was a red-hot tennis player.

Except for the size of the family, none of that is true anymore.

We lived in Norwood, Virginia, not very far south of Washington, D.C. Spring is a magical time of year in Virginia; I awoke to a morning filled with sunshine and birdsong. I lay there in bed for a while, too comfortable to make the effort to get up, enjoying the gentle warmth of the sun on my eyelids and the faint, sweet scents drifting up from the backyard garden.

If I close my eyes today, I can still smell those flowers. They were hyacinths, I think.

After a time, the clock on the table next to my bed gave a threatening click, and I reached over blindly to punch the switch to keep the alarm from going off. Then I opened my eyes to the beauty of the day. Sunlight poured in through the open window, and the crystal prism Steve had given me for my seventeenth birthday two weeks earlier to symbolize "a year that will be filled with rainbows" twisted and spun on the end of its thread, creating a multicolored kaleidoscope on the wall across from it.

Mine was an unusual room for a high-school junior. My best friend, Sherry Blaugrand, whose bedroom walls were covered with posters of rock stars, liked to refer to it as "Princess April's Chamber." The furniture in the "chamber" was composed of antiques handed down by my grandmother, Lorelei, when she sold her house. The four-poster bed and the matching chest of drawers were cherrywood, and an oval mirror in an ornate gold frame hung over the dresser. In one corner there was a rocking chair with hand-carved arms and a blue velvet cushion, and opposite that stood a camphorwood chest that my grandparents had brought back from a trip to the Orient.

But the room was not just a reflection of Lorelei. There was a bookcase crammed with my own favorite paperback novels and a stereo next to the bed with a record rack beside it. A shelf beneath the window was lined with tennis trophies, and on the dresser Steve Chandler's face grinned mischievously out at me from a borderless picture frame.

There was something about that grin that was contagious. I blinked sleep from my eyes and smiled back at the boy in the photograph. Then I let my gaze flick past him to the door of the closet. The Junior-Senior Prom was only four days off, and in that closet hung my first full-length formal.

Sitting up, I swung my legs over the side and got out of bed. As I passed in front of the window on my way to the bathroom, a breeze slipped in to ruffle the curtains, and the prism hanging from the curtain rod twirled gaily, spattering my cotton pajamas with rainbows.

I brushed my teeth, got dressed, and invested ten laborious minutes twisting my long blond hair into a sophisticated French braid. Then I got panicked about time and hurried downstairs. My mother and brother were already seated at the table in the kitchen, and our fat golden cocker, Porky, was positioned beneath it. Bram was busily burying his cereal under a layer of sugar, and Mother was too engrossed in the morning paper to notice. In front of her sat a coffee mug with I DO THE JOB WRITE printed on it. It was filled to the brim with thick, black liquid that looked like the residue from a tar pit.

"Anything new on the trial?" I asked by way of greeting.

"If there is, it's not in the paper," said Mother.

"I wish they'd get things settled so Dad could come home," I said. "You'd think at least they'd let him commute on weekends."

I got a glass from the cupboard and a carton from the refrigerator and poured myself some orange juice.

Mother raised her eyes from the paper and zeroed in on Bram. "Don't tell me you're putting sugar on that presweetened cereal!"

"Only a little," Bram said, pressing down on the mound with his spoon so it disappeared into a rising sea of milk.

"You don't need *any*," said Mother. "Not with Corrigan teeth! Last time you went to the dentist he found three cavities!"

As always, when things came down on him, Bram changed the subject.

"Can I sleep over at Chris's Saturday night?"

"I thought he was spending the night over here on Friday."

"He is," Bram said, "but Saturdays are two-for-one nights at Video Plus. We're going to rent all the 'Nightmare on Elm Street' movies."

"What's going to happen when you guys grow up?" I asked him. "Will you and Chris build houses next door to each other?"

"We're going to marry sisters," Bram informed me. "We'll live together, and our wives can take turns cooking."

"Sit down and eat some breakfast, April," said Mother. "You can't make it through till lunchtime on nothing but orange juice."

"I don't have time," I told her. "I'm running late today. Steve will be coming by for me any minute now."

As if in response to my words, a car horn beeped out front.

"What did I tell you!" I gulped the juice and plunked the empty glass down on the tabletop. "I won't be home till late. I've got practice after school."

In a matter of seconds I was out the door and halfway down the driveway. Steve's Honda Prelude was pulled up at the curb with the engine idling. I dumped my books in through the window to free my hands so I could open the door. When I climbed into the front seat beside him, Steve reached over and hauled me across so he could kiss me good morning.

The kiss missed my mouth and landed on the tip of my nose.

" 'Rapunzel, Rapunzel, let down your hair!' " he teased me, giving my crown of braids a threatening tug.

"Don't you dare pull those loose!" I shrieked in mock terror. "I'll never be able to get them back up without a mirror!"

"Not to worry, I'd never destroy such a masterpiece." He kissed me again, and this time his aim was better. "Mmmm —toothpaste and orange juice, my two favorite flavors."

"If you'd turned up three minutes later, I'd have tasted like cereal," I said.

"Your mom's got a campaign going for better breakfasts?"

"I don't know what it is with Mother," I told him. "She never used to get uptight with Dad out of town, but lately, whenever he's gone, she starts spoonfeeding us."

"What's it been now, anyway—a couple of weeks?" Steve asked.

"Longer than that," I told him. "Try three and a half."

"Then give your mom a break. No wonder she's edgy. Imagine if you and I were apart that long!"

Rotating the steering wheel with his left hand, he slid his right arm around me and pulled me against him. With a sigh of contentment I leaned my head back against his shoulder.

"You're right," I said. "Three weeks apart would be the pits. I hope we never have to be separated three *days.*"

Steve and I had been going together since Christmas. We had found each other at a tree-trimming party at Sherry's house. I use the term "found each other" because we didn't actually meet there. We'd been casual acquaintances since back in junior high, when we had been on the Student Council together because we had been presidents of our respective classes.

Even so, we had not really gotten to know each other. In high school we seemed to move along parallel paths, glancing across to say hi, but not brushing shoulders. We never seemed to have any classes together, and whenever Steve had A lunch, I had B lunch. Besides, our extracurricular activities were different. I was into tennis and cheerleading, and Steve was involved in speech and debate and school government. When I dated, which was often, it was usually the jocks, while Steve went out with brainy girls from the speech team.

That night at Sherry's party the girl's name was Valerie,

and I was with a teammate named Bobby Charo. Bobby and I were on the outs that evening. He'd been late picking me up, and in the car on the way to the party I had given him the silent treatment to retaliate. His response was to make a play for Valerie. Valerie grabbed at that opportunity to make Steve jealous, so halfway through the evening she and Bobby were draped all over each other as they danced in a shadowy corner of the Blaugrands' rec room, while Steve and I sat in front of the fireplace and drank cocoa.

Steve gestured toward our dates. "Well, what do you think? Is it possible they're trying to tell us something?"

"I couldn't care less what they're trying to tell us," I told him. "Bobby is free to dance with anybody he wants to. It's not like we're going together. He's just a friend."

The truth of it was, I was absolutely furious. I wasn't used to being treated so rudely. Bobby had been showing me so much attention at tennis practice that I had expected him to devote himself to me all evening.

Steve set down his cup and reached for my hand.

"Who needs 'friends' like those two? Come on, let's dance."

He pulled me to my feet and out onto the dance floor. It was obvious that he was a much better dancer than Bobby. Within minutes I was leaning comfortably into the warmth of his body, drifting effortlessly along to the slow, sweet beat of the music.

"I've always thought it would be neat to dance cheek to cheek," Steve murmured. "Now at last I've found a girl who's tall enough to do it with."

His cheek was smooth against mine, and his breath smelled faintly of chocolate, and a piece of tinsel from the Christmas tree was caught in his thick, dark hair. Over his shoulder the tree lights twinkled like red and green fireflies, and beyond that the fire filled the room with a golden glow. Magic was all around us, and I realized to my astonishment that I would not care if I never saw Bobby again.

When the song was over I started to go sit down, but Steve pulled me back.

"What do you think you're doing?" he asked in an injured voice. "Are you going to force me to dance with my chin in the hair of some midget?"

"A fate worse than death!" I said, laughing, and stepped back into his arms. I didn't leave those arms for the rest of the evening.

When the party was over and Bobby appeared dutifully at my elbow, Steve gave him a look that would have frozen the ears off an Eskimo.

"If we're swapping dates, then let's do it right," he said. "You take Valerie home, and I'll take April."

Later, when I described to Sherry what had happened, she said, "What did you expect? Who else would Princess April end up with but Prince Charming?" There was a note of undisguised envy in her voice. Sherry had had her own eye on Steve since the beginning of the school year.

Now, almost five months later, the magic had not lessened. In fact, with each passing day, it seemed to be growing.

"So what's the deal with your father?" Steve asked as we drove to school. "You've never explained why he's stuck up there in Washington. What's his connection with that guy who's charged with drug running?"

"Mr. Loftin is one of the bigwigs at Southern Skyways," I said. "He and Dad have traveled together on business trips to South America, but of course there's no way my father's involved in the drug scene. He wouldn't recognize cocaine if it was sprinkled on his cereal."

"Maybe the fact that he's straight is what makes him valuable," Steve suggested. "The defense might be planning to use him as a character witness."

"Your guess is as good as mine," I told him. "Dad hasn't been allowed to discuss it with us. Until he gets back, all we know is what we read in the papers."

Steve steered the car into the student parking lot. Then he and I got out and walked across to the school building. The first bell was already ringing as we stepped through the doorway, and that was the start of my last day at Springside Academy.

It was an ordinary school day, no different from any other. In world history, Mrs. Winnender (referred to behind her back as "Mrs. Wind-Without-Ender") delivered an hour's oration on ancient Rome. In English class, Mr. Peyton assigned us the whole last act of *Hamlet,* and we all groaned appropriately. There was a substitute teacher for algebra who gave us permission to do whatever we wanted just as long as we stayed at our desks and talked in whispers. Business as usual—nothing to prepare me for a crisis —nothing to set the stage for End of Our World Day.

Since Steve and I didn't have lunch the same period, I ate in the school cafeteria with Sherry and some other girls. Then, after lunch, my tennis partner, Jodi Simmons, and I went out to the gym to see if Coach Malloy had posted the seeding for the state tournament. He had, and we were pleased to find we were first in women's doubles and that I was first, and Jodi second, in women's singles.

Steve was waiting for me at my locker when the bell rang, and we coordinated our plans for the rest of the day. Steve had an appointment after school to get measured for his prom tux, but he said he'd be back to pick me up after tennis practice. Then, since he'd taken Shakespeare the year before, he offered to spend the evening explaining *Hamlet* to me.

"Catch you later," Steve told me as we split forces.

"Later," I responded with perfect confidence.

The first of my afternoon classes was Mrs. Guthrie's typing lab. I was taking the class at Mother's insistence, because, being a writer, she was convinced there was no future for people who couldn't type. That day there was a timed assignment that involved long columns of numbers, and I was concentrating so hard on increasing my typing speed that I almost didn't react when I heard my name called.

"April?" The voice broke into my consciousness. "April Corrigan, you're wanted in the counselor's office."

I glanced up then and saw the student messenger standing by Mrs. Guthrie's desk.

"Do you want me to finish the assignment first?" I asked.

"No, you'd better go now," the teacher said. "And take your things. You might not make it back before the end of the period."

More curious than worried, I gathered up my books and papers and pulled the dust cover over the typewriter. Keyboards were rattling away like a barrage of machine guns as I walked down the aisle between the rows of typing tables. Nobody dared lose momentum by glancing up at me. Even Sherry, whose desk was three in front of mine, didn't raise her eyes from her assignment sheet as I passed her.

I didn't get to say a single good-bye.

By the time I left the room, the messenger had long since gone, so I made my trek to the counselor's office alone. Except for a monitor stationed at the foot of the stairway and a girl who was getting a drink at the water fountain, the hall was empty. Without its usual cargo of aromatic teenagers, it smelled benignly of chewing gum and chalk dust, with a faint aroma of pot smoke near the boys' rest room.

The door to Mrs. Winnender's room stood partly open, and as I passed, I could hear her voice, wearier than it had been that morning, still rattling away about Rome in its era of splendor. Aside from that the only sound in the hall was the hollow click of my footsteps bouncing back from the rows of lockers that lined the walls.

I opened the door of the counselor's office and stepped inside. On a bench opposite the doorway two boys with bloody noses sat glaring at each other, obviously longing for a chance to continue their fistfight. Farther down on the bench sat a sullen redhaired girl, chewing gum like a riveting machine. The redhaired woman seated next to her was pretending not to know her.

None of them was waiting for me.

The secretary was busy talking on the telephone, and there did not appear to be anyone else in the room. Then, suddenly, the door to one of the inner offices swung open, and out stepped a person I had not expected to see there.

"Come along, April," she said crisply. "I've signed you out."

It was Lorelei.

2

Lorelei has never been your typical grandmother. Back in grammar school I couldn't wait for Grandparents' Day to roll around so I could show her off to my friends and teachers. Other kids would show up with plump gray-haired grandmas in polyester pantsuits, while I would arrive with a slim blond fashionplate without a line in her face.

So blinded was I by my pride in her that it wasn't until I was practically into junior high school that I began to realize that Lorelei was not very popular on Grandparents' Day. My teachers found her intimidating, and my classmates, defensive about their own soft, wrinkled grannies, thought her strange and unnatural. As for the grandmas themselves, they drew nervously away from her as though she were a visitor from another planet.

Their unfriendliness did not bother Lorelei in the slightest. In fact, she seemed to take it as a form of compliment.

The reason I was surprised to see her at school that day was that she and Mother had not spoken to each other for several weeks. This was not at all unusual for the two of them, who, although they were mother and daughter, had such totally different personalities that they were constantly at odds about one thing or another. The most recent area of conflict was Mother's refusal to take time off from the book she was working on to write press releases for Lorelei's current fund-raiser.

"What do you mean, you signed me out?" I asked her now. "I can't leave school. I have to stay for tennis practice."

"I'm afraid you will have to miss practice today," said Lorelei. "Your mother asked me to drive over here and get you."

"I thought you and Mother were mad at each other," I said.

"I can't imagine how you got an idea like that." Lorelei threw a pointed glance at the redhaired woman who was listening to our conversation with undisguised interest. "Come along, April. We will do our talking in the car."

Obediently I trailed her out to the visitors' section of the parking lot and climbed into the passenger's seat of her white Porsche. As I secured the seat belt across my chest, I said, "All right, we're alone now. What's going on?"

"I haven't the faintest idea," Lorelei said. "As I told you, your mother phoned me—she actually had me paged at the country club—and asked me to drive over to the school and pick you up."

"You didn't ask her why?"

"Of course I asked her why," said Lorelei. "She said she couldn't talk and would tell me later. She sounded so upset, I didn't pursue it. I canceled out of lunch and jumped into the car."

Since that took care of the only subject that either of us was interested in, we didn't talk much during the rest of the drive.

When we reached the house, there was a car in the driveway next to Mother's station wagon, so Lorelei was forced

to park her own car at the curb. She did this without com-
plaining, a fact that made me uncomfortable, as it empha-
sized the oddness of the situation. Lorelei was very protec-
tive of her Porsche and never willingly left it parked on the
street.

When we entered the house, my brother came bouncing
out into the entrance hall with Porky yapping at his heels.

Bram's eyes were shining, and his face was aglow with
excitement.

"The school let me come home early today!" he announced importantly. "And guess what else? We're going on
a mini-vay!"

"What are you talking about?" I asked in bewilderment.
"Mini-vay" was a term my parents had coined back in my
early childhood to mean a tiny vacation or a short family
outing.

Glancing past him into the living room, I saw Mother
seated on the sofa, talking with a man in his early forties. As
we entered the room, they turned to face us, and a chill of
apprehension shot through me as I saw the expressions on
their faces.

"Uncle Max!" I exclaimed. "It's been such a long time!"

"Hello there, April," said Max. "You're looking prettier
than ever." The fact that he wasn't smiling increased my
nervousness. In every memory I had of him, Max had a
smile on his face, wide and white, almost blinding in its
intensity. Dad told me that as boys growing up in Pittsburgh, he and Max had lived in adjoining duplexes. In bed
at night, Dad would rap on the paper-thin wall that separated their bedrooms, and Max would smile and rap back at
him. "I'd feel that grin come straight through the wall,"
Dad said, laughing. "It was like being hit by a double bolt of
electricity."

Without that smile Max's face was much less attractive
and etched with lines I had previously not been aware of.

"Lorelei," said Mother, "I'm sure you remember Max

Barber. He and George have known each other since childhood."

"I also recall he's an FBI agent," said Lorelei. "From the
vibes in this room, I gather this isn't a social call."

Instead of responding directly, Max glanced at Mother.

"I'll tell them myself," she replied to the unspoken question. She paused as though trying to decide how to word her
disclosure. "Children, something frightening happened this
morning. Somebody in the courtroom fired a gun at your
father."

In the silence that followed, the impossible statement just
hung there, the words too incomprehensible for any of us to
grasp.

Finally I managed to whisper, "You mean Dad's been
shot?"

"*No!*" exclaimed Mother. "Of course not! I'm sorry I
scared you. The shot was off target, and Dad wasn't hit.
Max drove down from Washington to break the news to us.
He didn't want us to learn about it from television."

Bram's face was so white that his freckles stood out like
polka dots. "Why would anybody want to shoot Dad?" he
asked shakily.

"To keep him from giving testimony," said Max. "I
promise you from now on he'll be heavily guarded."

"You captured the gunman, of course." Lorelei phrased it
as a statement.

"I'm sorry to have to tell you this, but we didn't," Max
said. "Incredible as it seems, nobody actually saw what happened. Court had just been adjourned for lunch, and the
aisles were jammed. The person who fired the shot was using a silencer, and since George wasn't hit, he didn't react
immediately. By the time the security people got the exits
blocked, most of the spectators had already left the courtroom."

"I don't understand," I said. "Why would anyone think
Dad—"

"We'll discuss that later," said Mother, cutting me off. "I want you to go up now and pack your overnight bag. We're going to go away for a couple of days."

"Where are you taking them?" Lorelei asked, turning to Max. "Surely it isn't safe for them to be with George."

"I have no intention of taking them to Washington," Max told her. "That's the last place George's family ought to be right now. I don't think they're in any real danger here in Norwood, but to be on the safe side, it would be best to get them out of the house."

I tried again. "But what can Dad possibly tell them—"

"April, please, don't ask questions," said Mother. "There just isn't time for that. Go up to your room and put some things in a suitcase. Max is going to put us up in a hotel tonight."

Feeling as though I had suddenly been handed a part in a grade B movie, I did as directed and went upstairs to my bedroom. The suitcase I used for sleepovers was in my closet, where I had stowed it after my last overnight at Sherry's. When I hauled it out and opened it, I discovered it had never been unpacked. It contained not only pajamas but last month's issue of *Seventeen,* a stamped envelope with an order form from a record company, the favorite purple sweatshirt I'd been searching the house for, and a pair of jeans I had thought I would never see again.

The clothes smelled moldy from having been closed away so long. I carried them into the bathroom and dumped them into the hamper. Then I went back to my room and stood staring at the suitcase, trying to figure out what I ought to put in it. I wondered if we would be staying at the Colonial Inn. If so, I should be prepared to dress up for dinner. The inn had a formal dining room where people ate by candlelight while a woman in an old-fashioned tea gown strummed on a harp.

I knew I ought to be frightened, but somehow I wasn't. The truth was, I couldn't believe this was really happening.

I took a white linen dress down from its hanger and put it in
the suitcase along with my good high-heeled pumps and a
pair of panty hose. Then I packed my good jeans, an extra
blouse, a change of underwear, pajamas, my toothbrush,
and my portable hair dryer. As I was getting ready to close
the bag, another thought struck me, and I rooted through
my bureau for my swimming suit. The public pool in Norwood had not yet opened for the summer, but the pool at
our town's best hotel was sure to be heated.

After I'd finished my packing, I carried my bag downstairs. Everybody else was gathered in the hallway. Mother
had a suitcase, and Bram, his backpack. A stranger looking
in on us at that moment would have thought we were setting off on a family vacation trip.

Bram had experienced one of his characteristic mood
swings and gone from fear and bewilderment to nervous
excitement.

"What about Porky?" he demanded, tugging at Max's
sleeve. "Can Porky come with us? He's never stayed at a
hotel!"

"Dogs aren't allowed in hotel rooms, Bram," Max told
him. "I'm sure, though, that your grandmother will look
after him for you."

"Lorelei doesn't like Porky," said Bram. "She says he
barks too much. I'll ask my friend Chris if Porky can stay at
his house."

"I don't want you contacting anybody," said Max. "This
is a secret getaway, like you see on television. No one can
make even one phone call. We don't want a single person to
know where you're going."

"But Porky can't stay in the house by himself!" Bram
objected.

"I'll see that he's taken care of," Lorelei assured him.
"There's a nice little kennel right down the street from my
aerobics class. I'm certain Porky will have a wonderful time
there."

Mother made a trip through the house to see that the doors and windows were locked, and then we went outside and got into Max's car. Porky tried to jump in after us, but Bram shoved him out.

"You have to stay here with Lorelei," he informed him.

Porky let out a sound that was half moan, half whimper. He was no more fond of our grandmother than she was of him.

"Call me tonight so I'll know where you are," said Lorelei.

Mother shook her head. "You heard what Max said."

"He didn't mean that you couldn't call *me!*" Lorelei protested. "For the love of heaven, Elizabeth, I'm your *mother!*"

"I'm sorry, but Liz is right, Mrs. Gilbert," Max told her. "She and the children are not to make calls to anyone. I'm sure you'll agree that their safety must take top priority right now."

He got into the driver's seat and started the car. As we pulled out into the street, I impulsively turned around in my seat and looked back through the rear window. Our house was positioned in the center of the glass like a painting in a frame, and the whole front yard was ablaze with the brilliance of springtime. The last of the red and yellow tulips, the first of the bearded iris, pansies, azaleas, and crocuses overflowed the flower beds. The purple leaf plum and the tulip poplar were at the peak of their bloom, and the whole side yard was one solid mass of pink dogwood.

I stared for a moment, implanting the scene in my memory. Then the car rounded a corner, and the picture was gone.

I expected Max to head straight for the Colonial Inn, but instead he drove us into the center of town. Then, to my added surprise, he pulled up in front of the Federal Building and turned into the underground parking area for official vehicles. He flashed a card at the attendant, who motioned

us through, and we descended a ramp to the lowest level of
the garage and pulled into a parking space next to a Volks-
wagen van.

A gray-haired man was seated behind the wheel. When
we pulled up beside him, he glanced across and nodded.
Then he got out of the van and came over to speak to us.

"I was starting to think I was being stood up," he said.

"It took longer than I expected to get the kids out of
school," said Max. He turned to Mother. "Liz, this is Jim
Peterson. For the next few days he's going to be your bodyguard."

"But I thought *you* were going to be staying with us!"
exclaimed Mother.

"I've got to get back to Washington," Max told her. "I
want to check on the security setup for George. I couldn't
leave you in better hands than Jim's. He's a former cop and
a pro at witness protection."

"Don't worry about a thing, Mrs. Corrigan," Jim Peterson said. "I've got a wife, three kids, and seven grandchildren. I know how I'd feel if anything happened to them,
and I'm not about to let anything happen to you."

The two men transferred our luggage over to the van.
Then they had Mother, Bram, and me get into the back.
There was a seat along either side, and Mother and Bram
sat on one, and I on the other.

"The vehicle switch is in case we were tailed," explained
Max. "That's unlikely, but we don't want to take any
chances." He leaned in through the open door, the charis-
matic smile back in place, and gave Mother's hand a reassuring squeeze. "Keep your chin up, Liz, and try not to
worry. When George agreed to work with us, we promised
you'd be safe."

He stepped back from the van and slid the door shut. The
windows in the back had been painted over, and we suddenly found ourselves in semidarkness.

Jim Peterson started the engine, and the van rumbled into life.

"Now can you tell me what's going on?" I asked Mother. "It can't be possible somebody meant to *kill* Dad! How much of a threat is the manager of an air freight office?"

"Dad is more than an office manager," said Mother. The light was too dim to allow me to see her expression. "There's a reason we haven't seen Max for over a year now. He's deliberately kept his distance to downplay their friendship. Ever since the last time Max was at our house for dinner, your father has been working secretly for the FBI."

3

We didn't stay at the Colonial Inn. Instead we continued driving for over two hours. By the time Jim Peterson finally brought the van to a stop in front of the Mayflower Hotel on the outskirts of Richmond, my eyes had grown so accustomed to its dark interior that it was a startling experience to step out into daylight.

"Is this where we're staying?" asked Bram, squinting up at the high-rise with that brown-eyed, blue-eyed gaze that so disconcerted strangers.

"This is it," Jim said. "We have a reservation for 'Peterson.' For the time we're here, we will all be using my name."

Although the Mayflower did not have the old-fashioned elegance of the Colonial Inn, what it lacked in atmosphere it more than made up for in size. We walked into a lobby as large as the auditorium at Springside Academy, with a back wall lined with boutiques and gift shops. While Jim was checking us in at the registration desk, a bellhop rushed to collect our luggage and a uniformed garage attendant parked the van. We rode up to the fourteenth floor in a futuristic, glass-walled elevator, and the "room" that had been reserved for us proved to be a suite, complete with a living room, two bedrooms, and two baths.

"Hey!" yelped Bram, as he bounded across the living room to open the glass doors leading out to a balcony. "April, come out and look! There's a humongous swimming pool!"

"It's a good thing, then, that I packed my suit," I said.

While Jim was tipping the bellhop, Mother sat down on the sofa, and I followed my brother out onto the balcony. Across from us, rows of identical porches jutted out from the opposite wing, their doors reflecting the low, slanted light of the late afternoon sun like a row of mirrors.

Bram hung over the railing to peer down at a patio area below us where a turquoise pool lay surrounded by yellow deck chairs. Only a few of the chairs were occupied, and the pool was empty.

"Rats!" Bram exclaimed. "I wish I'd brought my swim trunks!"

"I'm sure we can pick up a pair for you tomorrow," I said. "Maybe they even sell them in the hotel gift shop."

"I'm hot right *now*," Bram complained. "I don't want to wait till tomorrow. Why didn't Uncle Max say there would be a pool?"

I left him standing there grumbling and went back into the living room. By now the bellhop had gone, and our suitcases were lined in a row just inside the entranceway. Jim was in the process of securing the chain on the door, and Mother was staring with unfocused eyes at a painting on the wall across from her, looking as exhausted as if she had just put in a twelve-hour day at her word processor.

Jim regarded her with concern. "Are you okay, Mrs. Corrigan?"

"No," said Mother. "I'm feeling pretty shaky. And by the

way, don't you think you should call me Liz? Since we're sharing a suite, I take it we're supposed to be related."

"Right," agreed Jim. "I'm either your uncle or your father." He sat down on the chair across from her, and from my position behind him I could see the pink of his scalp peeking out through the wispy strands of gray and was suddenly, painfully reminded of my Grandpa Clyde. The brisk, no-nonsense voice was like my grandfather's also. "Bram, will you please come in here? We have things to talk about. We've got to establish some ground rules for our stay here."

When Bram came in from the balcony, his shirt was unbuttoned. He was evidently in stage one of preparing for the pool.

"Do you think they let people swim in shorts?" he asked hopefully. "I've got cut-offs in my pack that look sort of like swim trunks."

Mother started to answer, but Jim was ahead of her.

"I'm sorry, but you're not going to be able to go swimming here. It isn't the time of the year yet for family vacation trips. People who saw you would wonder why you weren't in school."

"Who cares!" yipped Bram. "There's nobody here who knows us!"

"That's probably true," Jim agreed. "Still, we're not going to risk it. If somebody's out to find you, he'll be casing out hotels."

"But there's no way for anybody to know we're in Richmond!" I protested.

"I hope you're right, but we can't be certain about anything."

"Please, do as Jim says without arguing," Mother told me. "He's not just being arbitrary, he's trying to protect us."

"Protect us from *what*? Somebody jumping in and drowning us?" I couldn't believe the turn the conversation had taken. "What are we supposed to do tonight in the dining room? Are we going to eat with napkins over our faces?"

"We won't be eating in the dining room," Jim told me. "We're going to have our meals brought up by room service."

"You mean you're going to keep us locked up like prisoners!" I gestured toward the telephone on the coffee table. "Next I suppose you'll be telling me I can't call my boyfriend to let him know he can't come over this evening."

"You already know the rule about phone calls," said Jim.

"But Steve and I have a date to work on an English assignment! It's bad enough that I wasn't at the courts after tennis practice. If Steve comes over to the house and nobody's there, he's going to freak out!"

"Calm down," said Mother. "It's not the end of the world. In a couple of days we'll be home, and you can explain everything."

"You wouldn't say that if it was Dad who was worrying!" I was becoming more and more frustrated every minute. "It's not as though Steve is going to tell anybody anything! All this cloak-and-dagger business is ridiculous!"

It was a good line to exit on, but I had nowhere to go. From what Jim had just said, we weren't even to be allowed in the corridor. The only refuge available was a bedroom, so I stalked into the closer of the two and slammed the door. Then I gazed about me, wondering what to do next. The room did not offer many alternatives. It contained two queen-sized beds, two dressers, and a television set with a coin box on top of it. Since I'd left my purse in the living room, I couldn't rent a movie, so I flicked on the set and punched into a regular channel. A rerun of *Facts of Life* appeared on the screen, and I threw myself down on one of the beds to watch it.

At first I expected Mother to come in after me to try to talk me into rejoining the group in the living room. After a while, though, I realized she wasn't coming and that I was

caught in a trap of my own making. I couldn't stay shut
away in the bedroom forever, but to walk back out without
being begged to do so would be the same as agreeing with
Jim's ultimatum.

I couldn't bear to do that when I was in the right. And I
was in the right, no question about it. There was no way
Jim, who had never even met Steve, could be a judge of
whether or not he should be trusted.

The *Facts of Life* show seemed to drag on forever. Finally
the episode reached its inevitable conclusion with Jo and
her boyfriend riding off on motorcycles. Then came a couple of commercials and a newscast. It was hard for me to
believe it was only six. I glanced across at the clock radio on
the bedside table and was surprised to see that there was a
telephone next to it. I had assumed the only phone in the
suite was in the living room, and it had not occurred to me
there might be extensions.

I stared at the hunk of beige plastic with its digit-pocked
face, feeling as Eve must have felt when she first saw the
apple. All I had to do was dial Steve's number, and I could
break our date and explain the reason. I knew he was home,
because his brother Billy was in Little League, and the
Chandlers always ate dinner early on game nights. A phone
call, drowned out by television, would not be discovered
until it appeared on our hotel bill. By that time we'd be
checked out and headed for home, and my one small act of
rebellion would not be an issue.

I was just preparing to reach across for the telephone,
when it burst into life with an accusative ring. The sound
was so unexpected that, without pausing to think, I
snatched up the phone.

I was all set to blurt out an automatic "Hello" when I
heard Jim's voice and realized he had taken the call in the
living room and we must have lifted receivers at the same
exact instant.

". . . well enough, all things considered," he was saying.

"If anybody was tailing us, the guy was invisible. Where are you calling from? Are you back in the office?"

The voice that responded belonged to Max. "I'm at my daughter's apartment, using her ultra-safe, unbugged phone. How are things there? Is Liz holding up okay?"

"As well as can be expected," said Jim. "Of course she's worried about her husband. Hang on a sec, there's something she wants to say to you."

There was a short pause, and then Mother said, "I want to talk to George, Max."

"I'll try to arrange to have him phone you tomorrow," Max said. "He's not here now. I'm making this call from Susie's place. George has a private room and a personal bodyguard. We can't let him call you from there, though. Too many people have access to the hotel switchboard, and it's open knowledge our witnesses are housed at the Farragut."

"But he *is* all right?" Mother pressed him.

"He's fine, believe me. After today the courtroom will be closed to spectators. The only people allowed in will be lawyers and jurors."

"I'd feel much better if I could just hear his voice," said Mother.

"I'll do my best to see that you hear it tomorrow. Now, please, get Jim back on the line again. There are a couple of more things I need to discuss with him."

There was another brief pause. Then Jim said, "Yeah, Max?"

"This is just between us," Max said. "Don't make any comments. A special delivery letter arrived here today for George. Thank God, we intercepted it before he got hold of it. If he'd read it, I doubt we could get him on the stand tomorrow. The language was graphic—the writer didn't stint on adjectives—and the threats weren't aimed at George as much as his family."

"You can't—" Jim began, and stopped.

"You're right, we can't withhold it indefinitely, but we can hang on to it for twenty-four hours. Usually I can talk George into anything, but he might pull out if he thought his family was in danger. We can't afford to do anything to rock the boat right now. The shit hits the fan as soon as our boy nails Loftin. He's knocking over the first in the line of dominoes."

"I guess that means we stay put for a while," said Jim.

"There's no way I want the Corrigans to step out of that hotel suite. The scope of this is bigger than we ever anticipated. If George has all the information we hope he does, he's got enough ammo to blow this ring to hell and back."

"I got it," said Jim. "So how about doing me a favor? Give Della a call and tell her I won't be home this weekend. We were planning on having our son's brood over for a cookout. Tell her to ask the kids to give us a raincheck. Maybe we can reschedule it for Memorial Day weekend."

"I'll tell her," said Max. "But you'd better not make any promises. There's no way of knowing how long you're going to be stuck there."

"However much time it takes, then that's what it takes," Jim said. "I knew when I took this job that it wouldn't be a lawn party. Like I told you, though, the old bod is giving me some problems. You're sure you don't want to send me over some backup?"

"You'll handle things fine," said Max. "You're a longtime pro. No need to double the guard when you're holed up in a fortress. I'll check in again tomorrow to see how it's going."

There were two sharp clicks, and then the sound of the dial tone.

I set the receiver carefully back on its cradle, trying to absorb the immensity of what I'd just heard. Up until then I'd thought of our situation as a drama made for television, crafted to fit into its allotted time slot. Now I was stunned to learn that no time limit had been set for it. Fragments of dialogue from the phone conversation churned in my mind, stirring up questions for which I had no answers. "As soon as our boy nails Loftin, the shit hits the fan." What could my father say that could have so much impact? What were the "dominoes" Dad was going to knock over, and how long a time had Jim meant when he'd said we would have to "stay put for a while"?

But the biggest question of all was, should I tell Mother? Was there anything to be gained by repeating what I'd heard to her? She couldn't discuss it with Dad until he called her, and by then he would already have learned about the letter. No, the best thing to do, I decided, was to keep what I'd heard to myself. Mother was upset enough without my making things worse for her, and besides, I wasn't too keen to admit I'd been eavesdropping.

There was a rap at the door, and Bram stuck his head in.

"Mom says to tell you dinner's here," he said. "Do you want to come out and eat, or are you still mad?"

"No, I'm not mad," I told him. "I was overreacting. Of course I'm going to come out and eat dinner with the rest of you."

I tried not to think about Steve arriving at an empty house. Instead I got up from the bed and went out to the living room, where I found that Jim had ordered prime rib for all of us.

4

As Max promised, Dad phoned Wednesday evening. The call came while we were eating, and Mother took it in our bedroom with the door closed, leaving her seafood casserole to congeal on her plate, while Bram and I sat fidgeting and waiting for our own turns. She stayed on the phone twenty minutes, and when at last she came back out into the living room, it was obvious she had been crying, and equally obvious Dad wasn't waiting on the line for us.

"We talked too long, and he had to hang up," she said. "The plan's been changed. We're not going home on Friday."

"But we have to!" Bram protested. "Chris is spending the night!"

"I'm afraid that's off," said Mother. "We're here for the duration. I'm not happy about it either, but we don't have a choice. Dad says it isn't safe to go home until the trial's over. April, I'm so sorry you'll have to miss the prom."

The prom! In all the excitement, I'd forgotten the prom!

How could I have spaced out the biggest event of the school year!

"Steve's chairman of the Entertainment Committee," I said miserably. "He's got to go to the dance whether I do or not."

"I'm sorry," Mother repeated. "I know how upset you are. We'll make it up to you somehow, honey, I promise."

"You can't," I said. "This is Steve's senior year and his last school dance. And the worst of it is I can't even let him know what's happened to me!"

"Have some dessert, it'll make you feel better," said Jim. He handed across a plate, and it slipped from his fingers, dumping a slice of cheesecake into my lap. "Oops—sorry about that. It's getting ready to rain. I can always tell when the joints in my hands cramp up on me."

"Let it pour!" I snapped. "At least we're not going to get wet! We're all sealed up in our super luxurious prison!" I stomped into the bathroom and sponged the white glop off my jeans (the only pair I had with me, I reminded myself bitterly). Then I fed quarters into the meter on the television and lay on the bed and watched old movies until bedtime.

In the morning Jim went down to the gift shop and bought a newspaper. The murder attempt on Dad hadn't rated a banner, but it did get a four-column headline across page three. The article identified Dad as "an employee of the airline, working as an undercover agent for the government" and disclosed that during the past eight months he had accompanied Richard Loftin on two flights to South America. Dad's testimony read that on both occasions they brought back cocaine. "Our suitcases were packed full of the stuff," he said. "We didn't claim the bags when we arrived in the States, so they didn't have to go through routine customs inspection. Airline employees confiscated the unclaimed luggage and placed it in airport lockers. Later it was removed and delivered to the dealers."

I read the article through twice, too stunned to assimilate it. I felt as though the man being quoted was a stranger. The gentle, conservative father I had known for seventeen years could not have been actively engaged in the traffic of narcotics! When Mother had told me that Dad had been working for the government, I had pictured him peeking and prying in logs and ledgers, and that in itself had been almost inconceivable. It had never entered my head that he had become so deeply involved that he had been a physical part of the smuggling operation.

"It's so out of character!" I said. "Dad isn't a risk taker. He'll even stop at a yield sign when both streets are empty!"

"Chalk it up to a master manipulator," said Mother. "Ever since they were boys together back in Pittsburgh, Max has been leading your father around by the nose."

I stared at her incredulously. "I thought you *liked* Max!"

"He's Dad's old buddy, so I've tried to like him," said Mother. "The truth of it is, I think all that warmth is a put-on, and I've always resented the influence he has over your father. Max is all the things Dad always dreamed of being— smooth and macho, spewing out charm and self-confidence. Even his line of work seems exciting and glamorous, a million times more exotic than managing a freight room. When Max offered Dad this chance to play the part of a hero, he grabbed it as though it were the brass ring on a merry-go-round. I did everything in my power to talk him out of it, but Max had him all fired up to be James Bond Two."

"But why would Max want Dad for a spy?" I wondered. "There must be Secret Service agents who are trained for that."

"The fact that Dad had no previous connection with the government was the very thing that made him so valuable," explained Mother. "He had been working at Southern Skyways for years. It was much more effective to use a man who was already a trusted employee than to try to plant an outsider in the inner circle."

"How much longer is the trial going to last?" I asked her. "I've got to be back in time for Steve's graduation."

"We can't possibly be here *that* long," Mother said confidently. "The hearings have been under way for a week now."

As things turned out, she couldn't have been more mistaken. We stayed cooped up at the Mayflower two and a half weeks. The novelty wore off quickly, and after just a few days we'd settled into a routine of unbearable monotony. I would wake in one of the two huge beds in the larger of the bedrooms, and for one brief moment, before I became fully conscious, I might forget that I wasn't in "Princess April's Chamber." Then I'd open my eyes, and reality would slam down on me. When I glanced at the bed across from me, there would be Mother, awake and staring at the ceiling. Bram, who shared her bed, would be lying on his back, snoring softly like a tea kettle on the verge of boiling. With no reason for getting up, Mother and I would continue to lie there, conscious of each other, but with nothing to talk about, until Bram woke up and we were able to send down for breakfast.

Our meals from room service were the high points of the day. Even I, who was normally not a breakfast eater, found myself waiting eagerly for the waiter to lift the cover from the hot plate so I could see if the eggs came with sausage or bacon. Jim gave us permission to order whatever we wanted, and Bram and I sampled every dish on the menu. Mother went off the deep end ordering seafood and even started having wine with her dinner. And all four of us hit the desserts like there was no tomorrow. By the end of the first week my jeans were uncomfortably snug, and by the end of the second I couldn't secure the top button and was forced to let my shirt hang out over the waistband.

But the hardest thing for all of us was a lack of activity. Bram was by nature a hyper kid who couldn't sit still ten minutes, and I was used to being on the go both physically and socially. Mother was accustomed to being at home by herself all day, but she was also used to spending those hours working. To be stuck without the word processor on which she did her writing was more frustrating to her than being deprived of her freedom.

Finally, in desperation, she started writing in longhand. She would sit at the desk in our bedroom, filling up pages of hotel stationery, oblivious to the shrieks of delight and the groans of disappointment that came from the contestants on Bram's favorite shows. Television was our only source of entertainment. While Bram watched his shows in the bedroom, Jim and I watched the soaps in the living room, and in the evening we all watched movies and sitcoms. For the eighteen days we were there, the only live people with whom we had contact were the maids who made up our rooms and the waiters who brought our meals.

In many ways the nights were even worse than the days. Although I always felt logy, I almost never felt drowsy. I would lie there in bed, waiting for sleep to come to me, trying to ignore the noises of hotel living. The rattle of pipes as toilets flushed in the bathrooms. The chatter of voices as people passed in the hall. Music and laughter, drifting up from the open-air bar in the patio under our window. The sounds of activity were intensified by the darkness and the fact that I was trying so hard not to listen to them. There were times when I almost imagined I could hear the creaking and groaning of beds in the rooms above and below us as their inhabitants shifted positions on unfamiliar mattresses.

Although Mother, Bram, and I were not allowed to go out, the hotel provided laundry service, and Jim got some extra clothing for us at a shopping mall. He also made regular forages down to the gift shop to pick up such necessities as deodorant and toothpaste, and on one embarrassing occasion, a box of tampons. And every morning and evening he went down to get newspapers. The moment he was back,

Mother snatched them from him and eagerly combed the pages for news about the trial. As the hearings dragged on, the articles kept getting shorter, and eventually they were bumped to the C section next to "Dear Abby." It wasn't until the jury retired to their chambers that the story again made an appearance in section A.

As soon as the verdict was in, Max phoned to tell us. He called at midafternoon, when I was out on the balcony trying to get a start on my summer tan. The sound of the phone was so unexpected that for a moment I simply stood there, too startled to react. Then I whirled and bolted back into the living room, where Jim already had the receiver to his ear.

"Hello?" he was saying. "Yeah, that's what we all expected. Do you want to tell her yourself, or do you want me to do it?" He paused for a moment, then handed the receiver to Mother. "It's Max. The jury is in, and the verdict is guilty."

Mother's face lit up like a neon light.

"Thank God!" she exclaimed as she grabbed the receiver from his hand. "Max, is it really over? Has George left for home yet?" As she listened to the answer, her smile lost its brilliance. "Well, of course his attorney will appeal, that's standard procedure. What does that have to do with George being kept here?"

This time she was silent much longer. Creases appeared between her eyes, and she started to drum her fingers impatiently on the coffee table.

Finally she said, "What you're telling me doesn't make sense. There's no way Loftin could have made those threats from prison." She paused. "Can't the letters be traced? Isn't that your job?" Another pause. "I suppose we have no choice, then, but I don't understand why you couldn't have told us sooner."

She hung up the phone, and Bram gave a squeak of excitement.

"Are we going home? Can I sleep in my room tonight?"

"I'm afraid not, honey," Mother said in a strange, tight voice. "Dad has received some threatening letters, and Max thinks we should stay where we are until they find out who wrote them."

"But Steve's graduation is this coming weekend!" I protested. "I have to be there for that and for the parties afterward!"

"I'm sorry," said Mother. "That's just not going to be possible."

"You promised!" I wailed.

"I didn't *promise* you anything. I simply said that I thought we would probably be back in time."

"So we're stuck here for life, just because of a few stupid letters! We don't even know they were written by somebody dangerous! There are all sorts of screwed-up kooks who hide in the woodwork and write weird letters to people whose names are in the newspapers!"

"Don't yell at me, April," said Mother. "I just can't take it. You're not the only one who wants to go home, you know. My book is due at the publisher's the beginning of August."

"So send it in late!" I shot back at her. "They'll publish it anyway! I'm the one who's had to miss everything—first the prom, then Steve's graduation—and now, for all we know, we could be stuck here all summer! Steve is going to think I'm never coming back! If Jim doesn't let me talk to him, I'm going to go crazy!"

I whirled and ran into the bedroom and slammed the door. Then I threw myself down on the bed and burst into tears. Mother was usually a reasonably straight-thinking person. It was hard to believe she was taking those letters so seriously. The trial was over, so why would anybody harm us? In fact, what proof did we have that we'd ever been in danger? A shot had been fired, but no damage had been done to anybody, so maybe the gesture had only been meant to scare Dad.

I don't know how long I lay sobbing into my pillow before I heard the sound of the doorknob turning.

A moment later I felt a hand on my shoulder.

"Go away!" I hiccoughed. "I don't want to talk to anybody!"

The voice that answered was not the one I expected.

"You don't have to," said Jim. "You've done far too much talking already. You've got a lot of growing up to do, April. You're a nice enough kid, but you're part of the Cinemax generation. You can't believe real-life stories don't always have happy endings, and you think of yourself as the star and the rest of us as bit players."

"That's not true!" I cried, glaring up at him through my tears.

"Then give some thought to your mother," Jim said brusquely. "She's worried about your dad, and she's hitting the wine too hard. She's in no condition to deal with your childish temper tantrums."

"This isn't a tantrum!" I struggled to keep from shouting at him. "Are you too old to remember what it's like to be in love!"

"My personal life is none of your business," said Jim. "*Your* personal life is *my* business when it puts you in danger. I didn't like what I heard just now in the living room. I want you to promise you're not going to call your boyfriend."

"I wouldn't have to tell him where we are," I said. "I could just let him know I'm safe and tell him I miss him."

"Absolutely not," said Jim. "It's out of the question."

"What harm would it do? You're being so unfair!"

"There's always the chance you might let something slip."

"So what if I did? Steve wouldn't repeat it to anybody. Or do you think every phone in this state has been tapped?"

"You're not to call your boyfriend," Jim said firmly. "I'm not going to leave this room until you've given me your promise."

"All right, I *promise,*" I told him. "Now are you satisfied?"

"I'd like to believe you mean that, but I don't think I trust you."

"What are you going to do about it, lock me in a closet?"

"I'm going to tell the operator not to put through any calls from this suite," said Jim. "I can't afford to take chances with a hysterical teenager."

He left the room, pulling the door closed behind him and leaving me lying there, seething with indignation. I could not remember ever having been so furious! Jim had no right to accuse me of being a liar! It was insulting to be monitored by the hotel operator, and I wasn't about to allow myself to be intimidated! Jim had forced me to promise that I wouldn't phone Steve, but I hadn't said that I wouldn't get in touch with him some other way.

Swept along on a rising wave of perversity, I jumped up from the bed and crossed the room to the desk. As usual, Mother had spent her morning working, and sheets of hotel stationery, covered with line after line of her neat, slanted handwriting, lay scattered across the desktop in a haphazard manner. I took a fresh sheet from the drawer and tore off the letterhead. Then I sat down at the desk and composed a letter.

Dearest Steve—

A note from your missing Rapunzel! I wish I were really the princess in that fairy tale and could let my hair down fourteen stories so my prince could climb up to me. I felt so dreadful standing you up for the prom. Now I've found out that I'll miss your graduation too. I'm so disappointed and miserable I just want to die. I wish I could say where I am, but I'm not allowed to. I'll explain everything when I get home. For now, just know I'm thinking about you every second of every day, and I miss you, miss you, miss you.

All my love,
"A"

After I'd completed the letter I reread it carefully. As far as I could see, it was totally innocuous, void of every shred of real information. Still, to play it totally safe, I added a postscript—"Don't show this note to anybody and destroy it after reading."

My next concern was how to get the letter delivered. I couldn't mail it in a hotel envelope with the name and address of the Mayflower printed in the corner. Another problem was that I didn't have a stamp. I thought about sneaking down to the lobby to buy one, but the only time I could do that would be after Jim was asleep at night, and at that late hour the shop was sure to be closed.

Suddenly I remembered the form for ordering records. I'd filled it out with Sherry the last time I'd spent the night with her and I'd meant to put it out the next day for the mailman. Then, for some dumb reason, I hadn't unpacked, and the suitcase with all of its contents had been stashed in my closet. I'd dumped out the musty clothing when I'd repacked, but I didn't recall that I'd ever removed the envelope.

My overnight bag was lying open on the luggage rack, and when I checked the side pocket, the envelope was in it. I managed to pry it open without tearing the flap and substituted my letter for the printed order form. Then I resealed the envelope, crossed out the address for Columbia Records, and wrote Steve's name and address in its place.

Late that night, after everybody was asleep, I tiptoed through the dark living room and unlocked the outer door. Then I took off the chain and let myself out into the hall. The brush of my bare feet on the heavy carpet sounded so loud in the empty corridor that I kept expecting a dozen doors to fly open and a chorus of voices to demand to know "What's going on out there?"

Of course that didn't happen. Nobody accosted me. I didn't even run into a drunken hotel guest staggering back to his room after a late-night party. I crept down the hall without seeing or hearing anyone and dropped the letter in the mail chute between the elevators. Then I returned to our suite, got back into bed, and slept more soundly than I had for a great many nights.

5

I mailed the letter in the dark, early hours of Wednesday morning and figured Steve was bound to receive it on Friday. In his neighborhood the postman made his rounds in the morning, and since Mr. and Mrs. Chandler both worked and Billy was still in school, it would probably be Steve who brought the mail in from the box, possibly upon his return from commencement rehearsal.

I spent most of Saturday picturing his face when he saw the printed form with the address scratched out and his own written in in my handwriting. By late afternoon I was telling myself, "By now he's got it. At this very minute he's probably sitting on his bed, reading it over and over, so glad and relieved to finally have had some word from me."

To me, that thought was what Mother's wine was to her; it lifted my spirits and gave me a momentary high. I really needed that lift, because our living situation had become more depressing than ever since my showdown with Jim. We addressed each other politely ("Please, pass the salt"— "Would you mind if I switched channels?") but aside from such conventional civilities, we had exchanged few words since our confrontation on Tuesday. Mother didn't seem to notice our strained relationship. During the day she scribbled away at her desk, and in the evening she was so mellowed out and drowsy that she usually went to bed before Bram and I did.

It wasn't easy to avoid Jim's company in such close quarters, but I made it a point to do so as much as possible. Instead of watching soaps with him in the mornings, I watched Bram's game shows in the bedroom, and despite the fact that the weather was damp and muggy, I spent a lot of time sitting out on the balcony, reading paperback novels and watching hotel guests splash in the pool fourteen floors below me.

On Saturday afternoon Jim followed me out there.

"Stop being childish," he said. "Let's call a truce."

"I don't know what you're talking about," I said coolly.

"Don't give me that. You've been pulling a sulk for three days now, pouting like a three-year-old whose father's forbidden her to play in the street."

"You've been *treating* me like a three-year-old!" I retorted. "Besides, you're *not* like my father, my father *trusts* me! I told you I wouldn't phone Steve, and you didn't believe me. I don't like having people call me a liar, and I'll never forgive you for talking to the hotel operator."

Jim was silent a moment, digesting that statement. Then, to my great surprise, he said, "I apologize. Actually, I never did contact the operator. I was worried that you were getting ready to do something dumb, and telling you that was the only way I could think of to stop you."

"I'm not stupid," I said.

"You don't have to be stupid to be dumb," said Jim. "My granddaughter, Monica, is just your age and nuts about a kid with a Harley-Davidson. Monnie's normally as level-headed as they come, but she turns into somebody else when she gets with this boyfriend. She's got this idea that the two of them together are invincible. She rides on the back of that motorcycle without wearing a helmet, while he steers with one hand and chugalugs beer with the other."

"That's not only 'dumb,' " I said. "It's just plain crazy."

"Sure, it's crazy, but Monnie doesn't think so. She's thinking with her glands instead of her brain right now. Anyway, like I said, I'm sorry I hurt your feelings."

The apology made me ashamed of my own rude behavior. When I looked at Jim with his thinning hair and his weathered face, with the laugh lines and worry lines fanning out from the corners of his eyes, he reminded me so much of the grandfather who had died when I was twelve that I felt a sudden, overwhelming surge of affection.

"I'm sorry too," I said. "I was pretty horrid. I didn't mean that crack about your being old."

"If you'd said it today, I'd have had to agree," Jim said wryly, lifting his hands and grimacing as he flexed them. "At least in my line of work I don't get writer's cramp. I pity your mother if she ever gets arthritis. There's no way hands like these could keep pushing a pen all day."

"She doesn't usually write in longhand," I told him. "That's probably one of the reasons she's so bummed out at night."

"We're all bummed out," said Jim. "We're going stir-crazy. Why don't I see if I can pick up a few board games? Do you and your brother play Scrabble? Or what about Yahtzee?"

"Bram can't spell well enough for Scrabble," I said. "He likes Monopoly, though, and Family Feud."

"If they're not in the shop downstairs, I'll check out the mall," Jim said. "None of us needs another night of the boob tube."

After he left, I remained outside on the balcony, fighting the guilt I felt at not having come clean with him. I knew that I should have told him I'd sent Steve a letter. On the other hand, there was really nothing to be gained by that, and it wasn't as though what I'd done had put us in danger. There were ways for people to trace a phone call, but after listening to Mother's conversation with Max, I realized that even the FBI, with all their sophisticated technology, couldn't trace a letter that was sent through the mail.

I stayed outside awhile longer, trying to sort things out in my mind until, around 4 P.M., the overcast dissolved in a drizzle and I was forced to move back inside. There I found Bram in the living room, sprawled on the floor, watching TV through half-closed eyes like a zombie.

"Jim's gone out," he said. "He went to the mall."

"He's gone to buy some games we can play tonight."

"I wish we could go swimming," Bram commented wistfully. His round face suddenly brightened as an idea struck him. "If Jim's at the mall, then he won't be back for a while. It's starting to rain, and the pool won't have anybody in it."

"No way," I told him firmly. "We've got to live by Jim's rules." The moment the words were out, I felt like a hypocrite. I decided that when Jim got back I'd make my confession. The worst he could do in response was to bawl me out again, a small price to pay for dumping a weight off my conscience.

For lack of anything better to do until his return, I plunked down on the sofa and gave myself over to the Saturday Afternoon Movie, an adventure story about an ill-fated wagon train lost in the Arizona desert. For the next half hour Bram and I sat in silence, watching as the cast was reduced by a third by a smallpox epidemic and listening to a frontier woman scream her way through childbirth.

The newborn infant had just been kidnapped by Indians when I heard a knock at the door, and a voice called out, "Housekeeping!" Hauling myself up from the sofa, I went over and looked out through the peephole. There in the hall was the familiar, uniformed figure of one of the hotel maids, standing next to a cart piled with linens and cleaning supplies.

"The maid is here to make up the rooms!" I called to Mother, who was at work at her desk in the bedroom. "Shall I tell her to come back later after Jim gets back?"

"She's running so late, we can't ask her to wait," said Mother. "Besides, I'm dying for a shower, and we're out of clean towels."

So I opened the door and immediately wished that I hadn't. I stood there with one hand circling the knob and the other poised in readiness to undo the chain lock, experiencing the unsettling feeling that something was wrong. The woman who stood in the hall appeared anything but threatening. She was slender and tall, with blond hair and very dark eyes. The fact that I didn't recognize her wasn't surprising, as most of the hotel staff was off on the weekends and part-time workers substituted for the regulars. The maid wore the regulation blue shirtwaist dress with MAYFLOWER embroidered across the breast pocket and was manning the usual pushcart loaded with cleansers. True, her dress hung loose and was a little too short, hitting her just above her kneecaps, but that wasn't all that strange either, since if the woman only worked on Saturdays and Sundays, she might have borrowed a uniform from a full-time employee.

"What's the matter?" Bram asked me. "Why are you standing there?"

"Nothing's wrong," I told him, feeling like an idiot. Still, I continued to hold the door, not liking to appear foolish, yet oddly reluctant to open it the rest of the way. I wasn't able to pinpoint what was disturbing me and finally decided that it had to be the woman's eyes. I'd heard people use the term "black" in regard to eye color, but usually when you looked closely at someone whose eyes were described as black, you discovered that they were actually a very dark brown. This woman's eyes did not fall into that category. They were literally black, so the pupils were lost in the irises, and they dominated the rest of her face completely.

"Then why don't you open the door?" Bram persisted.

"That's what I'm doing," I told him, and slid back the bolt. At that precise instant I knew what was making me uneasy. My attention had been so caught by the maid's strange eyes that I had not taken in two other odd things. Her cheeks and chin were darker than the rest of her face, and her eyebrows were a different color from her hair.

I must have projected my panic at that discovery, because before I could move, she hurled herself forward, ramming the door so hard with the side of her shoulder that I found myself sliding back like an inefficient doorstop.

"Bram!" I yelled. "Come quick! Help me hold the door!"

"What do you want to do that for?" Bram asked casually, his eyes still glued to the flickering screen of the television set.

"Mother!" I shrieked. "Come fast! I need your help!" I couldn't believe the incredible thing that was happening. No cleaning woman would strong-arm her way into a hotel suite! Yet that was exactly what this woman was doing. The door was slowly and steadily being forced open, and I couldn't resist the strength being used against me. Everything seemed to be happening in slow motion. Mother had emerged from the bedroom and was hurrying toward me, but a million miles of floor space still lay between us, and I knew that she was not going to reach me in time to help me.

Then, through the widening gap between the edge of the door and the frame, I caught sight of Jim at the very end of the corridor, striding purposefully along with his arms filled with packages. A moment later the sacks were flying through the air and Jim was racing toward me with his left arm extended like a battering ram and his right hand fumbling frantically beneath the flap of his jacket. The next thing I knew, the maid had spun to face him, and Jim was shouting, "April, shut that door!" The sudden release of pressure accomplished that for me, and the door slammed closed with a crash that rattled the windowpanes. I shoved the bolt into place and punched the lock in the center of the knob, and then just stood there trembling, weak and shaken with shock and terror, my knees so rubbery they threatened to buckle under me.

By this time Mother had reached me and was braced against the door, although she obviously had no idea what was happening. From out in the hall there came a thump and a curse, followed by a pop like the sound of a cork coming out of a champagne bottle and the crash of the linen cart slamming into the wall.

"What's all that racket?" yelled Bram, scrambling up from the floor, belatedly realizing something exciting was happening.

"Stay back from here!" ordered Mother. "Who is that person, April? What in God's name's going on here? That wasn't any *maid*!"

"She's not even a woman!" I said shakily. "She has five o'clock shadow, and she's wearing a wig that doesn't match her eyebrows. She—I mean, *he*—tried to shove his way into the room. If Jim hadn't come when he did, that guy would be *in here*!"

In the corridor outside our room there was now only silence, an unnatural silence more frightening than the sounds of conflict.

Cautiously, Mother moved to put her eye to the peephole.

"What do you see?" I whispered after a moment.

"Nothing," she said. "But that doesn't mean he's not there. He could be standing out of my line of sight, flattened against the wall right next to the doorway. And Jim—I don't see *him*—he isn't there either." She raised her voice and called out, "Jim, are you out there?" When nobody answered she backed away from the door, clutching my arm and dragging me back along with her. "We've got to get out of range. If that man has a gun, there's nothing to keep him from firing it through the door."

"But Jim may be hurt!" I protested. "We've got to get help for him!"

"We're not going to open that door," Mother said firmly. "I'll call the front desk and tell them there's been a fight in the hall outside our room and we need Security to come up and check things out here."

It was probably less than five minutes, but it seemed like an hour before the security guard arrived and announced himself.

"Keep back," Mother cautioned. "We can't be sure who it is." She crossed to the door and again peered out through the peephole. "The chain lock's on, and I'm keeping it on," she said loudly. "What's going on out there? Is anybody hurt?"

"There doesn't seem to be anything wrong," the man in the corridor told her. "Whatever it was you heard, the disturbance is over."

"You mean there's nobody out there?" Mother asked incredulously.

"There's no one here and no indication of a problem. Actually, there aren't many guests on this floor right now. We hosted a convention this week, but it was over yesterday, and most of the people checked out last night or this morning."

"The hall can't be empty," I whispered. "I *saw* Jim there. And we both heard him fighting with the man who was dressed like a maid. It doesn't make sense, unless"—a thought occurred to me—"unless the man tried to escape and Jim ran after him."

"I hate to phone Max, but I guess I'll have to," said Mother.

"Uncle Max will be mad if you do," Bram piped up nervously. His face was white, and his lower lip was trembling. "He told us we couldn't call anybody, even Lorelei."

"I couldn't care less how mad he gets," said Mother. "Jim's disappeared, and we have no way of knowing what's happened to him. It's Max's responsibility to see we're protected, and if Jim is in trouble, then Max needs to deal with *that.*"

She called Max first at his office and then at his home, and finally ended up leaving a message on his answering machine. Then we settled ourselves to an evening of tedious waiting. The drab, gray afternoon skies slid into twilight and then into darkness without the grace of a sunset. Lights went on in the windows of the wing across from ours, but the night was too damp for people to be out on the patio, and an eerie quiet replaced the usual bustle of social activity in the party area under our windows. Mother didn't want to open our door to room service, so we dined on cheese and crackers and Bram's stash of candy bars, while outside our balcony doors the rain kept oozing down in a halfhearted drizzle, streaking the glass with slivers that looked like tears.

When Max arrived at last it was three in the morning. Although none of us was in bed, Bram was asleep on the sofa and Mother and I were dozing in chairs in the living room.

One glimpse of Max's grim face dispelled all my drowsiness. It was clear that he hadn't come with reassuring news.

"Have you talked to Jim?" Mother asked him.

Max shook his head. "We can't afford to wait to hear from him either. Get packed as fast as you can so we can get out of here. In another ten minutes this place will be swarming with cops, with the media perched on their shoulders like a bunch of vultures. I don't want you people interrogated by the city police, who don't know your situation and may leak your identities."

So we stole away in the night like escaping criminals. With Mother steering my sleepwalking brother by the shoulders, we took the service elevator down to the kitchen, where we groped our way through a maze of counters and stove tops. The darkness was broken at erratic intervals by the nervous flicker of dials on microwave ovens, and we left the building by a door that led to a service ramp.

Max's car was parked behind the garbage bins at the back of the hotel. The odor of rancid meat and spoiling produce contrasted strangely with the damp, clean smell of the night as we loaded our bags in the trunk and got into the car.

Once we were out on the freeway, Max turned in his seat. "You said he was dressed as a maid. Did you see his face?"

"He was wearing a wig, so his hair was covered," I told him. "I think, though, it must have been dark, because he had dark eyebrows. And his eyes were so black they looked like they didn't have irises."

"I know who that is," said Max. "His name's Mike Vamp. I should have guessed that he'd be the one they'd send for you."

6

The sky in the east was just beginning to turn pink when we completed the sixty-mile drive to Williamsburg and Max pulled into a parking space in front of a motel on the edge of town. He got out of the car and unlocked the door of one of the units, and the rest of us followed him inside.

The room was dimly lit, and it took me a moment to take in the fact that there was a man stretched out on one of the two double beds. Then he sat up, and I saw that it was my father.

"Dad!" I cried, and hurled myself into his arms.

He hugged me back so hard I thought my ribs would crack. Then he stood up and held out his arms to Mother.

"Oh, George!" she exclaimed. "Thank heaven, you're really all right! I've been so frightened for you!"

"That goes both ways," said Dad, holding her close and reaching out his other arm for Bram.

Max closed the door and carefully relocked it. "The big reunion can wait for later," he said. "There are things I haven't told you yet, Liz."

Mother turned in Dad's arms. "What sort of things?"

"Come sit down, honey," Dad said gently, drawing her down beside him on one of the beds. "There's something important we're going to have to discuss."

"Loftin's case is being appealed," Max told us. "That means that in less than a week he'll be out on bail. It also means that if the judge decides there was a mistrial, George will have to testify all over again. He's still in serious danger, and so are the rest of you."

"But we can't keep living in hotels forever!" I exclaimed, horrified by the thought of returning to the Mayflower.

"Of course you can't," agreed Max. "That was an emergency measure, and it served its purpose, but now you need more permanent protection. Have any of you heard of the Federal Witness Security Program?"

The color left Mother's face. "Oh, Max, no way! You're not about to get us involved in *that*!"

"The program's run by the U.S. Marshals Service," Max continued, ignoring her outburst as though he had not heard her. "It's supposed to be highly successful. Over fourteen thousand people have been relocated and helped to start their lives over in a safe environment."

"Helped to *start their lives over*!" Mother repeated incredulously. "George and I are happy with the life we *have*! We love our home, we have friends and careers, our children are happy in their schools—how can you suggest we begin life over at this point?"

"What is this?" I asked in bewilderment. "What program are you talking about?" I couldn't recall ever seeing Mother so upset.

"The Witness Security Program is just what the name implies," Dad explained. "It's designed to provide protection for people whose lives are in danger because they've blown the whistle on federal criminals. The program relocates those witnesses and their families. They're secretly moved to a different part of the country and given new identities so nobody can trace them."

"I don't want to move!" cried Bram. "Then I can't play with Chris!"

"And what about Steve!" I exclaimed. "I won't leave Steve!"

"I know this is tough," said Dad. "I'd give the world if I hadn't gotten us into it, but the fact of it is, we *are* in it, and there's no pulling out. You know about the letters that I've been getting. After what happened today, we have to take them seriously."

"The person who wrote those letters could be bluffing," I said. There was no way I was going to agree to leave Norwood! "That man who tried to shove his way into our hotel room might only have been planning to put a scare into us. There's no way we can be sure he intended to hurt us."

"Mike Vamp doesn't play pattycake, April," said Max. "He's one of the most notorious hitmen in the country. It's not just because of his name that he's known as 'the Vampire.' He follows the scent of blood as though he's got a hunger for it."

I closed my ears to that statement. "I won't leave Steve!"

"I'm afraid you're not going to have much choice," said Max. "There's something I haven't told you. We *did* find Jim tonight."

"I don't understand," began Mother. "Then why did we have to—"

"The reason I was in such a rush to get you out of the Mayflower was because I knew it was due to be invaded by police." Max paused and then continued. "Jim was shot in the head. His body was crammed in a linen closet at the end of the hall. He was carrying a gun, but he never got to use it. Apparently he wasn't able to get it out of his holster."

For a moment we were all too stunned to react.

"His hands," I finally whispered. "He had arthritis in his fingers."

"Then he should have known better than to take on this job," Max said. "The man was a former cop, he wasn't any neophyte." He placed a hand on Dad's shoulder, and although he wasn't smiling, his voice had a reassuring warmth to it. "I've got to get back to Richmond and see to things there. If I make it home by tonight, I'll call you from Susie's place. Tomorrow I'll get the relocation paperwork started. The sooner we get you out of Virginia, the better."

After he left, Dad went over and locked the door again. Then he came back and tried to put his arms around Mother.

"What happened tonight was tragic, but Max is right," he said. "Jim Peterson was a professional who acted irresponsibly. If he had a physical problem, he should have said so. If he couldn't do the job, he shouldn't have taken the assignment."

"George, I don't want to hear this. Jim was our friend." Mother pulled free of his embrace and turned to Bram and me. "Children, get into bed and let's all try to sleep for a while. Maybe, when we wake up, this will make more sense to us. Either that, or it will all turn out to have been a nightmare."

Of course, that didn't happen, but impossible as it seems, we did sleep heavily, as though we had been drugged by some gigantic tranquilizer with residual effects that lingered in our systems long after we awakened late in the morning. We spent the days that followed sprawled across our beds, leafing through magazines and watching the same soap operas and nonsensical game shows that we had watched at the Mayflower. There was a question I knew I ought to be asking myself, but it was too painful to contemplate, so I let it slide away. My mind felt fuzzy, unfocused, disconnected from my body. When I got up to switch channels or to go to the bathroom, I felt as though I were groping my way through fog, and once I slammed into the corner of an open dresser drawer and never even realized I had hurt myself until I was standing in the shower that night and glanced down to see a large purple bruise on my hip.

I realize now we were all in a state of shock. In my mind, of course, I knew that Jim was gone, but on a deeper level I didn't believe it. Every time I heard a car pull into the parking lot outside our motel room, I half expected the door of our room to pop open and see him come striding in with his arms filled with board games.

The account of Jim's murder rated only two paragraphs in the *Richmond Times-Dispatch,* but there was a lengthy obituary in the *Norwood Gazette,* which we found at a news-stand a block from our motel. I read it as though it was one of Mother's novels, a fictional story about an invented char-acter. It listed as survivors a wife, two sons and a daughter, and a large assortment of grandchildren, but I wouldn't allow myself to think of them as people, just as a meaning-less list of names without faces.

If I could have attended the funeral it might have been different. That ceremony gives death a stamp of authentic-ity, like the words "The End" on the final page of a novel. When Grandpa Clyde dropped dead of a heart attack in the middle of a golf game, I couldn't accept that fact until I went with my parents to the funeral home and saw the flower-decked casket with my grandfather in it. Only then did his death become reality to me, and only then was I able to start my grieving.

Since we couldn't go to Jim's funeral, we tried not to think about it. The day came and went, a slate gray day that was humid and heavy with rain clouds, and I knew that if Jim had been there his hands would have been aching. We closed off the sight of the day by drawing the drapes across the window and spent it as we did every other, reading and watching television, while outside the rain started falling, gently at first, and then progressively harder, on the roof, on the sidewalk, on the parking lot and, for all we knew, back in Norwood, on Jim Peterson's grave.

Max had not assigned us a replacement bodyguard, and he had not strictly forbidden us to leave our motel room. He had suggested that we go out as infrequently as possible, so we confined our outings to places like motel coffee shops and pizza parlors, and occasionally, in the evenings, we went to the movies. We'd been given a list of motels at which Max had made reservations for us, and at checkout time each day we left one motel and took a cab to the next. Every evening Max phoned us from his daughter's apartment to make sure we were safely resettled.

On the third night he told us we could expect a representative from the U.S. Marshals Service the following day. Rita Green, a sharp-featured woman in a polyester pantsuit, arrived at midafternoon. She settled herself in a chair in the corner of our motel room and studied our faces as though she were casting a play and we were actors auditioning for parts.

"I'm here to discuss relocation arrangements," she told us. "I assume that Max has explained the procedure to you."

"Actually we've been told very little," said Dad. "Please fill us in on how things are going to be handled."

"The first step, which we're working on now, is to fix you up with new identities," said Rita. "There are several possible ways of going about that. We're obtaining yours by the 'dead infant' method, Mr. Corrigan. With that, we search county birth records for a child who was born in approximately the same year you were but who is now deceased. We then apply for a copy of the birth certificate. Since records of births and deaths are not commonly cross-referenced, there's seldom any problem obtaining a duplicate."

"What about the rest of the family?" Dad asked her. "They're going to have to have the same last name I do."

"Since it makes no difference what your wife's maiden name was, we'll obtain her birth certificate the way we do yours," Rita said. "Then we can have a marriage certificate made out in your new names and planted at a bureau of public records. Of course, in the case of the children, the birth certificates will need to be falsified so their last names will be the same as yours and their mother's. Once you have your birth records, you can apply for other forms of identification like voter registrations and Social Security cards under your new identities. After that it's a simple matter to get a driver's license, which is actually the most important document of all."

"What about putting the children in school?" asked Mother. "Won't they need to have transcripts and inoculation records?"

"We'll falsify those as we do the marriage certificate and have them mailed directly to your children's new schools from a small private school in Vermont that we use for that purpose. There are people there who work with us on school transcripts. They have more 'former students' than any other school in the country."

"You mean our grades won't count anymore?" Bram asked hopefully. "Can all my Needs Improvements be changed into Excellents?"

"That's the sort of thing we try *not* to do," said Rita. "The transcripts should be a true reflection of your abilities. If your sister is poor in math, for example, and the math teacher at her new school decides to look up the grades she was making at her old school, we don't want her transcripts to make her out to be a math whiz. The less attention you draw to yourselves, the better. You don't want anything that's going to make people suspicious."

"Where are you going to be sending us?" asked Dad.

"That hasn't been decided yet," Rita told him. "In fact, that's the principal reason I'm here today. We want to put you someplace where there's as little chance as possible of your running into people who knew you before. Because of that, I need to know something about your backgrounds."

"I was born and grew up in Pittsburgh," Dad said obligingly. "That's where my relatives live, what there are left of them. By that I mean there's an aunt and some cousins. My parents and brother were killed in a car wreck the summer after I graduated from high school. For the next few years I drifted, not caring much what I did, trying one job after another, the way kids do. When Liz and I met, I was working at a resort in the Catskills. I've never been west of the Mississippi River, and I've never been farther south than we are right now."

"What about you, Mrs. Corrigan?" asked Rita.

"I'm an only child and grew up in Norwood," said Mother. "My mother still lives there and is very active in social and civic affairs. Apart from her, I don't have any close relatives, and except for the years I spent at Duke University, I've never lived anyplace other than Virginia."

"It sounds as though the West Coast might be a good location for you," said Rita. "It's easy for people to lose themselves in California. It's such a big state, and people keep coming and going there, so nobody bothers to question where anybody comes from."

"I don't really think that's a good idea," said Mother. "I might be recognized by librarians and English teachers."

Rita seemed disconcerted. "Do you have some connection with the California school system?"

"Liz is an author," explained Dad. "She writes books for children. Last year she won the California Young Readers Medal and made an acceptance speech at a state librarians' convention."

"Do you make many such appearances?" Rita asked Mother.

"Only at conferences of educators," Mother told her.

"That's a dangerous kind of exposure," Rita said, frowning. "No matter where we place you, your kids will be in school. All it takes is one teacher who's heard you speak, and word will be out that you're not the person you're supposed to be."

"I'm supposed to be giving a talk next month," said Mother. "How can I let the conference people know I won't be there?"

"We'll take care of that. Just give us a name and phone number." Rita turned to Dad. "Do you have any other questions?"

"Where will we get the money to live on?" Dad asked her. "How can I find a job if I don't have references?"

"We'll try to fix you up with something," said Rita. "We keep on the lookout for businesses that can be bought up inexpensively for our witnesses to operate. If you're the owner and manager of your own small business, nobody will have any reason to ask you for credentials."

"You mean I have no choice about what line of work I'm in?" Dad sounded as though he couldn't believe what he was hearing.

"Not much of one, I'm afraid. It depends on what's available."

"That doesn't sound very encouraging," Dad said grimly. "Any business that people are selling for peanuts isn't too likely to have much potential as a money-maker."

"We'll give you some cash to tide you over," said Rita. "In the meantime we'll see about liquidating your assets. I'll have papers drawn up for you to sign that will give our department the authority to handle the legalities. What do you own besides your house and furniture?"

"Two cars," Dad said. "A Volvo station wagon registered in Liz's name and a Chrysler sedan registered in mine. Jointly we own some shares of mutual fund, an income-producing utility stock, and a batch of CD's. My broker, John Scarbrough, is with the Dean Witter company. I also have retirement plan holdings built up at Southern Skyways, but I guess it's too much to hope I can get my hands on those."

"We'll have an attorney file papers to claim them," said

Rita. She paused. "Are we set, or do you have more questions?"

"I have one," Mother told her. "What about my mother? I haven't had any contact with her for weeks now."

"Max told me he's been in touch with Mrs. Gilbert," said Rita. "He offered her the option of making this move with you. She said she didn't feel she was in any danger and didn't want to leave her friends and activities."

"But we can't just disappear from her life!" exclaimed Mother. "She's stubborn and independent, but we're her *family*! What if she were to get sick or be hurt in an accident? She has to know how to reach us in an emergency."

"You'll just have to trust there won't be an emergency," said Rita. "As things stand now, you're the ones in danger, not your mother. You can't go into this program without breaking ties with people back home. It's hard, I know, but there isn't any alternative."

Bram spoke up suddenly. "What will happen to Porky?"

"Porky?" Rita repeated, regarding him blankly.

"My dog," said Bram. "My grandmother put him in a kennel. By now he's probably scared I'm not coming back for him."

"I'm sure your grandmother will take care of your dog," said Rita. She started to look away and then turned back again. "Is it a trick of the light, or are this child's eyes different colors?"

"It runs in the family," said Mother, immediately defensive. "My father had one blue eye and one brown eye."

"I'm afraid this is going to create a problem," said Rita. "Something this unusual will attract attention."

"Maybe I can wear dark glasses?" Bram suggested, sidetracked momentarily from the subject of Porky.

"Yes, for the present that's the best we can do," said Rita. "As soon as possible, though, you'll have to get contacts."

"Contacts!" Bram squeaked in horror. "I don't want contacts!"

"You won't have to wear them forever," Mother consoled him.

"How long?" I asked. "How long are we going to be gone?" The talk about Dad going into business and Bram and me starting new schools had been very disturbing. Why should we have to consider such unlikely possibilities? I'd assumed that the appellate court hearings would take place that summer. Surely that meant we'd be back in Norwood before school started.

Before Rita could respond, Bram exploded into tears.

"I won't wear contacts!" he shouted, going suddenly hysterical. "I don't want things stuck in my eyes, and Lorelei can't have Porky! He's *my* dog, not *her* dog! She doesn't even like him!"

The scene that followed was one of such emotional chaos that there was no more opportunity for sensible discussion. That night, however—after Bram had wept himself dry, after Rita had left to go back to Washington, after a dinner of carryout Chinese food and an evening spent watching sitcoms—I lay in bed, surrounded by my sleeping family, watching the play of lights on the wall across from me as cars sped along the highway in front of our motel. It was only then, thinking back on that strange conversation, that I realized the question I'd asked had never been answered.

7

Rita was back again in five days. This time she brought some official-looking papers in a folder that contained among other things four birth certificates and a marriage certificate.

The name on my father's birth certificate was "Philip Weber," and my mother's was "Ellen Paul." The marriage certificate was made out to show their true wedding date.

"At least we can celebrate our real anniversary," said Mother.

Bram's new birth certificate gave his name as "Jason Weber," and mine showed me to be "Valerie Weber," a name that I instantly hated. Not that I had ever been any too crazy about my real name. I'd always thought it sounded like an ingenue on a soap opera. But I knew there was no way I could ever be comfortable as "Valerie." When I heard that name the picture that leapt into my mind was of Steve's old girlfriend draped all over my own date, Bobby Charo, at Sherry's Christmas party.

"I will *not* be a 'Valerie,' " I said. "That name has bad vibes for me. Why can't we choose our own names?"

"Names are the least of our worries," Rita said shortly. "Our main concern is to get you people relocated. A major effort is being made to find you, and we want to get you transferred as quickly as possible."

"What's happened now?" Dad asked warily.

"Your mother-in-law had a phone call. The man identified himself as Mrs. Corrigan's editor. He told Mrs. Gilbert a movie producer wanted to buy the film rights to one of her daughter's books."

Mother's face lit up with the first real smile in weeks. "Did he say which book they want? What studio is it?" When Rita didn't reply, her excitement faded. "I take it you don't believe the call was legitimate."

"We *know* it wasn't," said Rita. "We called your publisher. The editor who was supposed to be trying to reach you was away on vacation. Nobody in the office knew a thing about a movie offer."

"Of course not," Mother said with quiet acceptance. "I can see now that the whole thing had to be a setup. A movie offer would have come through my agent, not my publisher, and neither of them would have tried to reach me through Lorelei. I don't think they even know what my mother's name is."

"A man like Vamp knows all the angles," said Rita.

"I don't like this," said Dad. "How soon can we get out of here?"

"You leave tonight," Rita told him. "It's all taken care of. I have you booked on a six P.M. flight to Florida."

"Florida!" Dad exclaimed. "That doesn't make sense. The drug trade in that state is the highest in the country."

"Vamp knows that too," said Rita. "It will work in your favor, because it will be the last place he'll expect us to send you. You'll land at the Sarasota-Bradenton Airport, but your final destination will be Grove City, fifty miles east of there. You're to travel in pairs, and your reservations have been made in the names of 'Freeman' and 'Gross.' That way, your tracks will be covered. Neither 'Corrigan' nor 'Weber' will appear on the passenger list."

Up until then, life had seemed to be stopped in a holding pattern like a frame of a broken movie reel. Now, abruptly, the film was running at triple speed, and in one brief moment we were jerked into frantic motion. For the next ten minutes we dashed about, grabbing up clothing, unplugging the hair dryer, and tossing our scattered belongings into suitcases.

We were ready to walk out the door, when Rita said, "Wait a minute. Something has to be done about Valerie's hair."

At first I didn't take in who it was she was talking about. Then, with a start, I remembered that *I* was Valerie.

"What's wrong with my hair?" I asked nervously.

"It's much too eye-catching. The color and length will make you stand out in a crowd. We're going to have to cut it before we leave here."

"No!" I cried. "I've been growing my hair for years!" My hands flew up protectively to cover my head. "I'll wear a wig or a scarf, but I'm not going to cut it!"

"It's much too long to fit under a wig," said Rita. "As for a scarf, nobody wears scarves in the summertime. Most physical characteristics can't be changed, but we can change the length of your hair, and it's important we do it."

"Mother!" I cried in anguish. "You aren't going to *let* her?" But even as I spoke, I knew it was hopeless. Mother had never worried about appearances, and her own short hair was cut in a blow-dry style that Lorelei and I had always agreed looked terrible.

I wasn't given time to argue my case. Within minutes I was standing in the bathroom with a towel draped over my shoulders and my eyes screwed shut so I wouldn't have to watch in the mirror as Rita hacked off my beautiful hair with fingernail scissors and Mother gathered it up and put it in the waste basket. Then we piled into Rita's car, a compact too small for five people, and sped back along the freeway toward the Richmond airport. The wind stroked the back of my neck with alien fingers, and despite the heat of the day, I found myself shivering.

During the drive Rita issued a string of admonishments about what we were to do once we arrived in Grove City. When we reached the airport, she pulled into a loading zone and kept the engine running while she distributed our plane tickets and handed Dad the folder of official documents. Then she wished us luck and drove away quickly, leaving me with the feeling that she was grateful to be done with us.

Once inside the airport, we paired off and proceeded on to the gate as we had been instructed. Mother and I entered the metal detector through one doorway, and Dad and Bram through another, and we sat at opposite ends of the waiting area, counting the minutes until flight time and trying to behave as though we didn't know each other. When the boarding call came, Dad and Bram went first, jumping up from their chairs and hurrying to the front of the line. Bram was having one of his hyper spells, hanging on to Dad's hand and bouncing along excitedly like a rubber ball on the end of an elastic band.

Mother and I hung back and fell into line with some late-arriving passengers. When we reached the door to the ramp we displayed our boarding passes and waited while the attendant examined them. He seemed to be taking a great deal longer than necessary, and I felt a sudden chill of apprehension. What would we do, I asked myself, if there was a problem with our tickets and we were asked to show identification? Although we were carrying documents made out in two different names, neither of them correlated with the names on our plane tickets.

As it turned out, I needn't have worried, for there wasn't

a problem. The attendant tore off the tops of our tickets and handed back the stubs.

"Enjoy your flight," he said with a friendly smile and waved us down the ramp and onto the plane.

By the time we entered the cabin, Dad and Bram were nowhere in sight, having taken seats at the back of the aircraft. Mother's and my seat assignments were toward the front, and we stashed our luggage in the overhead compartment and settled ourselves into the middle and window seats in the seventh row. Several more last-minute passengers hurried on board, flushed and breathless as though they had just run a marathon, and then the doors were closed and the flight attendants cruised the aisles, checking to see that everyone was wearing a seat belt.

A few minutes later Richmond lay far below us, a mosaic of rooftops, punctuated by brilliant blue swimming pools. The plane continued to climb until the city's highways had been reduced to a network of overlapping lines with black dots creeping along them like sluggish ants. Then, in an instant's time, the earth vanished completely, buried beneath a layer of marshmallow clouds, and we and our fellow passengers were alone together in an infinite expanse of open sky.

Mother reached over and gave my hand a squeeze.

"We've made it, honey," she whispered. "We're safe at last."

"You really do believe that?" I returned the squeeze, momentarily forgetting that I was mad at her.

"Of course," she said reassuringly. "And just think, we're going to Florida! What a wonderful place to take an extended maxi-vay!"

She was making such an effort to act lighthearted that I tried my best to respond with the same sort of cheerfulness. "I wonder if it's like the TV commercials, beaches and palm trees and everybody gulping orange juice."

"That sounds good," said Mother. "I wouldn't mind a

glass right now. Here comes the girl with the drink cart, maybe she'll serve some."

When the stewardess reached us, Mother ordered her orange juice spiked with vodka, which was something I had never known her to do before. I asked for a Coke, and the freckle-faced girl who sat next to me in the aisle seat ordered a Sprite.

"I like Coke better," she confided, wrinkling her nose. "I'm scared, though, of what might happen if we hit rough air. My mother bought me this dress just to make the trip in, and Coke's so hard to wash out if it spills on your clothes."

"I'm not wearing anything elegant enough to worry about," I said, having had no time to change out of my jeans and T-shirt.

"I see what you mean," said the girl, observing me critically. "My mother says people ought to dress up when they travel. That sure is a far-out haircut. Do you call it a shag?" She didn't wait for an answer. "I'm Abby Keller. I'm going to visit my dad and his wife for the summer." Then she asked the inevitable question, "What's your name?"

I froze for a moment, unable to come up with an answer. Although I could no longer call myself April Corrigan, I was not yet Valerie Weber, the identity I would assume once we landed in Florida.

"April Gross," I said finally, settling on a compromise. "Gross" was the surname printed on Mother's and my tickets.

"Oh, gross!" the girl exclaimed rudely and burst out laughing. "Do people tease you? I know my friends would tease *me*. Do they say, 'Oh, here comes that *gross* girl?' "

"A name's just a name," I said shortly. "People get used to it." Except when it's a name like Valerie, I added silently.

"Where are you going?" asked Abby. "To Sarasota?"

I nodded, feeling progressively more and more uncomfortable.

"I wish that's where I was going to be staying," said Abby. "It would be nice to live on the coast where the beaches are. My dad and his wife live in Dullsville. That's not really its name, of course, but that's what I call it. Can you believe the only movies they get there are so old you can already rent them as videos?"

I glanced across at Mother and saw she had finished her drink and fallen asleep with her head propped against the window. Beyond the double pane of glass the clouds were the color of smoke, and the sky was beginning to dissolve into gentle darkness. Mother's face was illuminated by the overhead reading light, which accentuated the rounded curve of her cheek. With nothing to do but read and eat and watch television, she, too, had put on weight during our confinement. That, and the angle at which the shadows fell, blunted her features and gave her for the moment the look of a stranger. This was not the author Elizabeth Corrigan; the woman dozing beside me was Ellen Paul Weber.

In the seat on my right, Abby continued to chatter.

"I bet Dad and Margaret don't even own a VCR. They probably don't even sell them in that hick town. If my folks had to get a divorce, you'd think the least my dad could have done would have been to move someplace exotic like Miami or West Palm Beach. But no, he moved to Dullsville to be with Margaret. Then after she got him to marry her, she didn't want to leave, because her daughter's got one more year of high school. Besides, Margaret's sister and *her* family live in Dullsville, and Margaret can't get along without all her relatives. Are your folks divorced? Is that why your dad's not with you?"

I mumbled some sort of noncommittal reply. Then, to my relief, the stewardess who had come by with the drink cart reappeared with a cartload of dinners on plastic trays. They didn't look appetizing enough to wake Mother up for, but I accepted one for myself and was pleased when Abby did, too, as I hoped that meant she'd stop talking and concentrate on eating. I underestimated my seatmate, however, for while I gnawed my way through a gummy chicken-noodle casserole, Abby continued to rattle along, undaunted by the food in her mouth, filling me in on every unpalatable detail of her parents' divorce and remarriages.

Finally, in self-defense, I gave up on dinner, put my seat into a reclining position, and closed my eyes. Incredibly, Abby finally took the hint and fell silent. I focused on the hypnotic roar of the engines, and the next thing I was aware of was a voice on the loudspeaker asking passengers to fold up their tray tables and check their seat belts in readiness for our descent into the Sarasota-Bradenton Airport.

When I opened my eyes I saw that Mother was also awake and had hauled herself up into a sitting position. As soon as the plane had taxied to a stop at the gate, we collected our bags from the storage compartments over our seats and joined the line of passengers leaving the aircraft. We emerged into warm, damp air filled with unfamiliar fragrances, descended a set of portable stairs to the ground, and crossed a short stretch of runway to the terminal, which was brightly lit and churning with activity. The door through which we entered opened into the baggage area, where a revolving belt was preparing to spew out luggage. Abby, who had popped out of her seat the moment the plane touched the ground, was there ahead of us with her mouth already in motion. With her stood a middle-aged couple whom I could only assume were her father and the detested Margaret.

Since we had not checked any luggage, Mother and I continued on across the lobby to a set of double doors at its far end. A few minutes later we were joined by Dad and Bram, who had left the plane through a door in the tail section. Bram seemed calmer, but his eyes were overly bright, and he did not show the slightest sign of drowsiness.

"You're not wearing your sunglasses!" Mother said accusingly.

"It's dark!" Bram protested. "You don't wear shades at night!"

"You'll have to until you get your contacts," said Mother.

"It's my fault," said Dad. "I spaced it out. There's been so much else on my mind I forgot to make him put them on. A car is supposed to have been left for us in the long-term parking lot. Rita gave me the license number, so let's see if we can find it."

We found the dented green Plymouth without much difficulty and made the drive to Grove City in just over an hour. Rather than the metropolis its name suggested, the "city" turned out to be a town with one main street that bisected a three-block business district. This downtown area was composed of small shops, a movie theater, a bank, a mom-and-pop grocery, and a J. C. Penney's. All the buildings were dark, and along each block, widely spaced street lights mottled the sidewalks with alternating pockets of light and shadow. The only indication that the town had a nightlife was a cluster of cars assembled in a parking lot next to a neon-lit building called the Cabbage Palm Bar.

According to the information in our folder, the house that had been purchased for us was on Lemon Lane, set back from the road with a mailbox in front that said "Jefferson." A hand-drawn map showed Lemon branching out from Orange, which intersected Main Street at Cypress Circle. We cruised back and forth along Main Street, looking for street signs, and finally somehow found ourselves on Orange Avenue. From that point on we faced even more of a challenge, for although there was a succession of tiny dirt trails leading off into underbrush, it was all but impossible to tell the roads from the driveways.

Dad selected one of these at random for the simple reason that it matched the position of a road that was marked on our map. We inched our way along it, straining to make out the numbers on houses that were hidden at the back of heavily wooded lots. It was Bram who spotted the mailbox with the name Jefferson, and Dad turned the car into a driveway that bridged a drainage ditch and wound its way back through a maze of trees and bushes, ending at last at the edge of a rickety carport that leaned forlornly against a small frame building.

He shut off the engine, and quiet descended upon us.

"Well, here we are," he said, his voice unnaturally loud in the sudden silence. "This is home sweet home, so let's check it out."

We got out of the car and climbed the steps to the porch, boards creaking beneath our weight in outspoken protest. Dad fumbled around in the darkness hunting for a keyhole, and finally got the door open. A wave of heat came rolling out to meet us, thick with dampness and the faint, sickly odor of mildew. It made me think of a locker room at a sauna with soggy towels left souring too long in hampers.

Dad switched on the overhead light, and the living room of our new home sprang into being, narrow and uncarpeted and unfashionably furnished with a sagging sofa, mismatched coffee and end tables, and a couple of overstuffed, underhung nylon armchairs.

"Max is playing a joke," I speculated hopefully.

"It could be worse," said Mother. "At least, I *suppose* it could."

"I wish Porky was here," said Bram. "I bet he'd like it."

Then Mother started laughing, and the rest of us joined her, not because what my brother had said was funny, but because you either laughed or you had to cry. We stood in that awful room and howled till our sides hurt, imagining Porky's ecstasy at being allowed on the furniture, which was something Mother had never permitted back home. Then we walked through the house, flinging open doors and peering into bedrooms, joking and making rude comments until we were teetering on the edge of hysteria. There were six tiny rooms—the living room, a kitchen, three minute bedrooms, and a bathroom—and each was in some way

worse than the room before it. Ceilings were cracked and
stained, plaster was flaking and pipes were leaking, two bedroom windows were broken, and when we turned on the
light in the kitchen an army of cockroaches frantically
scampered for cover.

"Who wants which bedroom?" asked Dad, and our
laughter stopped.

"We're not really going to stay here, are we?" I asked
him.

"We don't have a choice," said Dad. "The program's provided this. We're not in any position to make further de-
mands of them."

"George—" Mother said and caught herself. "I mean
Philip—" The strange name seemed to reverberate through
the room. "Philip," Mother repeated, trying out the sound
of it. "It's going to take me a while to learn to call you
that."

"Ellen, dear," Dad said gently, putting his arms around
her. "It doesn't make any difference what we call ourselves.
We're still the same people we always were, isn't that right,
kids?"

Bram and I nodded in automatic agreement. We *were* the
same people we always had been, *weren't* we? Still, in the
instant before I fell asleep that night, I remembered a carefree girl who used to sleep in a room fit for royalty, secure in
the knowledge that princesses live happily ever after.

I missed that girl, and I desperately wanted her back.

8

It was a miserable night.

To begin with, it was hot—overwhelmingly hot—the kind of hot that gives that word new meaning. Not that I was used to cool summers. Back home in Norwood we turned on the air conditioner at the beginning of June and kept it running nonstop until into September. There, at least, we'd *had* an air conditioner. Not only did our house in Grove City not have air-conditioning, it didn't even have fans to move the air around.

Besides that, the house had been closed up and baking in the sun for so long that it seemed to have absorbed the heat like a sponge and to now be radiating it back from walls, floors, and ceilings. My stifling bedroom had only one tiny window, and even when I cranked it all the way open, the heavy growth of trees and bushes along the side of the house cut off any breeze that might have existed.

Although I was so exhausted I dropped off to sleep immediately, I tossed restlessly all night, and my sleep was rampant with dreaming. In one especially vivid dream I was playing tennis and Bobby Charo was across the net, lobbing balls at me. We were playing with fireballs, and when I attempted to hit one it zoomed through my racket, leaving charred strings dangling like strands of blackened spaghetti and the handle searing my hand like a cast-iron skillet left too long on a stove burner. So intense was the heat that I started to melt as though I were ice cream, with liquid running down my legs and dripping off my ankles to form puddles on the hard clay surface of the court. At that point I heard a cheer and glanced up to see that the bleachers on either side of us were filled with students from Springside. Sherry was shrieking and waving and shouting encouragement, and Jodi was screaming instructions I couldn't understand. Steve was there too, cheering right along with them and looking spectacularly handsome in the red and white striped rugby shirt I'd given him for Valentine's Day.

The fact that I now had an audience made me play harder, and the heat of exertion was added to that of the tennis balls. The spectators seemed to grow more and more excited, but still I could not make out what it was they were shouting to me. Then, suddenly, a name rang out distinctly, and to my horror I realized that it wasn't my name. It was Bobby my friends were rooting for, because he was their classmate! To them I was just a visitor from Florida who was messing up their tennis court by melting all over it.

I awakened from that dream feeling sick and shaken, as if my disillusionment had occurred in real life. It took me several minutes to cut loose from the nightmare and to remember where—and, particularly, *who*—I was. When I did I drew a deep breath and opened my eyes to find that the pale light of dawn was seeping through the window and the first day of my life as "Valerie Weber" had started.

I lay there watching the room grow steadily lighter until I could make out the watermarks on the ceiling and the starburst of cracks in the wall across from my bed. My hips and shoulders ached from the lumpy mattress, and my sweat-dampened skin felt uncomfortably clammy in the morning air. I knew that to fall back asleep again would be impossible, so I got out of bed, got dressed, and went out to face the morning.

Moving quietly past the open doors of the other two bedrooms, I went down the narrow hall to the front of the house. I had some sort of crazy idea that the magic of sunlight might have caused a transformation there. Of course, that hope was short-lived, as daylight did nothing to improve the appearance of the living room. At least at night, by the glow of an overhead bulb, we had not been able to see cobwebs nestled in corners of the ceiling or the greasy marks unwashed heads had stamped on the sofa cushions. Now those were all too apparent, along with the little piles of mouse droppings littering the floorboards and the faded blue of the curtains drooping despondently at the windows.

Home sweet home, I thought wryly, and felt like crying.

Too depressed to continue, I opened the door and stepped out onto the porch. In contrast to my experience in the living room, I was pleasantly surprised by the world outside. The air held the scents of blossoming trees and overripe fruit, and the bushes that lined the driveway and had appeared so mysterious and formidable in the dark were, in the light of morning, a lush green backdrop for brilliant orange flowers. A rabbit was hopping across the yard, squirrels skittered up and down tree trunks, and an invisible chorus of birds was singing lustily in branches high above my head. Even the heavy underbrush that cut off the view of the road had a pleasant junglelike quality, like something out of a National Geographic travelogue.

Having nothing else to do until the others woke up, I descended the steps and walked down to the end of the driveway. Once there, I could see no reason not to go farther, and after considering a moment, I turned to my left and started back along Lemon Lane in the direction from which we had come the night before.

As I walked I considered the reason for our out-of-the-way location. It was apparent to me now why we'd had such a hard time finding the house. Not only were there no intersections for street signs, but there were no curbs on which house numbers could be displayed. The only indication that there were houses back behind the undergrowth was an occasional mailbox positioned next to a driveway. Obviously we'd been placed where we were deliberately, in an attempt to make it difficult for people to locate us.

The moment I reached Orange Avenue, everything changed, as though I had suddenly crossed some significant boundary line. Sidewalks abruptly materialized out of nowhere, and houses sat side by side on residential lots. I immediately felt more comfortable, like a traveler in a foreign country who discovers to her relief that the natives speak her language. Halfway down the first block I came upon a hospital, set in among the houses as though it was one of them, and two blocks farther I saw, on the opposite side of the street, a flat-roofed building with a sign that said GROVE CITY SECONDARY SCHOOL.

Secondary school? I thought, puzzled. What exactly did that mean? Was a "secondary school" a junior high or high school? I crossed the street and walked slowly along the pavement next to the building, trying to peer in and see what lay behind the windows. The rooms were dark and the glass was placed at an angle that permitted little view of anything but blackboards. The few clues I did find were oddly contradictory. On a windowsill there stood a row of geography books that looked as though they were geared to classes in middle school, but the wall of another classroom held a chart of symbols that seemed to be intended for a high school chemistry class.

Spurred on by my curiosity and beginning to enjoy the challenge, I rounded the corner of the building and continued on back to find out what lay behind it. I discovered a softball field and a small gymnasium, and back beyond that, a chain link fence enclosing tennis courts.

Long before I caught sight of the courts themselves, my ears picked up the sound of a ball being smacked rhythmically back and forth by a pair of rackets. The court in my dream sprang to mind, and I could almost see the high stacks of bleachers and the rows of familiar faces gazing down at me. The memory lost its impact when I came opposite the fence and was able to get a look at the couple who were playing. They were young and blond and looked like brother and sister, the boy bearing no resemblance to Bobby Charo. While Bobby was dark and wiry, this boy was tow-headed and had a heavy-chested build more appropriate for a quarterback than for a tennis player.

I went in the gate and took a seat on the spectators' bench. The couple continued to play without interruption, but during a break between games the boy glanced over at me and acknowledged my presence with a nod and grin. He was by far the better of the two players, for the girl was slow on her feet and looked exhausted. It was easy to see that the boy was holding himself back in order to keep his opponent from becoming discouraged. He took the first game but let the girl take the second. Then, with a few strong serves, he nailed down the set.

Appearing more relieved than disappointed, the girl started scooping up balls and putting them in the can.

"Hey, don't tell me you're calling it quits?" the boy called to her.

"Darned right I'm calling it quits! This is a farce!"

"Oh, come on, Kim, be a sport! You've just begun to fight!"

"You heard me—*no*! I'm all fought out, and I mean it."

"What a copout!" The boy turned to at me. "Hello, over there. I don't suppose you happen to be a tennis player?"

"I used to be," I answered, returning his smile. "I'm afraid right now I'm pretty out of condition."

"How about hitting a couple of balls for fun?"

"I'd like to," I said, "but I don't have my racket with me."

"You can borrow Kim's since she doesn't want to play anymore." He turned back to the girl. "You wouldn't mind lending it, would you?"

Kim pulled a kerchief out of the pocket of her shorts and wiped her face. She was perspiring heavily, and her hair was plastered to her head in tight, damp ringlets.

"Be my guest," she told me. "That is, if you're a glutton for punishment. I warn you, though, you'd better be prepared for the slaughter. My cousin Larry is captain of the tennis team. The rest of the guys are out of town or have full-time jobs, so he drags me here every morning so he can practice slamming balls at me. I'm scared to death I'm going to get decapitated. If you've got a death wish, take my racket and go for it."

"I'd like to give it a try," I said, trying to sound casual, although it was all I could do to keep from hugging her. It had been two months since I'd had a chance for exercise and every muscle in my body was screaming for action.

When I first walked onto the court, Larry set me up with a few easy balls to see if I could return them. It took only a couple of minutes of rallying for him to begin to realize that I was not the Sunday player he had expected.

"Hey, you're not bad for a girl!" he exclaimed in surprise. "Do you feel like playing for points? I promise to go easy."

Not bad *for a girl!* How I hated that condescending compliment! Steve would never have dreamed of making such a comment.

"Sure," I said. "Why not? Can you keep score? I'm afraid I haven't reached that chapter in the rule book."

I served the next ball with all my strength and watched it go zinging past him like a bullet. He looked so astonished, I could hardly hold back my laughter.

"Fifteen–love!" I called. "Are you ready for the next one?"

Larry moved back a few steps and squared his shoulders and suddenly started to play with true intensity. He was fast and strong and had a killer of a backhand, and when he pulled out all the stops he played like a maniac. After three close sets (I lost two but won the third) my heart was pounding in triple time and my legs were trembling, but I felt more alive than I had since leaving Norwood.

"You're good!" Kim said admiringly when I collapsed on the bench, as breathless and sweaty as she had been an hour earlier. "I'm Kim Stanfield, and my cousin is Larry Bushnell. You can't be from around here, or I'm sure we'd know you."

"I'm Val Weber," I told her, impulsively creating a nickname for myself. "We just moved here from Durham, North Carolina." Rita had told us to say we came from a state that was near Virginia so our accents would seem appropriate for our fabricated background.

"Are you going to be going to school here?" Larry asked me. Although he was trying not to show it, he was winded also.

"For the fall semester," I said. "I don't know about after that. Does secondary school mean junior high or high school?"

"It's both," said Kim. "Grove City has only two schools, the elementary school and the secondary school. There aren't enough kids who live here to fill up a middle school, so the seventh and eighth grades are thrown in with the high school."

"You'll like it here," said Larry. "This will probably surprise you, but we have the best high school tennis team in the state. We don't have enough big guys to make up a football team, so everybody who does anything plays tennis."

We sat on the bench for a while, resting and chatting,

until I suddenly realized how high the sun was. The cool of dawn had given way to the heat of morning, and I could already tell that the day was going to be a scorcher.

"I've got to get going," I said. "I took off while my folks were still asleep, and I didn't leave a note for them."

"I have to go too," Kim said without enthusiasm. "A relative's visiting, and I've been handed the job of entertaining her."

"Do you want to play tennis again tomorrow?" Larry asked me. "I'm working part time this summer in my father's lumber yard, but early morning is the best time to play anyway. Any later than ten and the heat's too heavy."

My heart gave a little jump of surprise and pleasure.

"That sounds great," I told him. "Let's meet here at seven."

Suddenly the world seemed brighter than it had been. I'd still have given anything to be back in Norwood, but at least I'd met some people and lined up a tennis game. Knowing that tennis was a popular sport in Florida made the thought of spending a semester there more tolerable.

When I got home another surprise awaited me. A second car was parked beside the Plymouth in the driveway, and when I entered the house I was greeted by the smell of coffee.

I found my parents and brother at the table in the kitchen, eating a carryout breakfast imported from McDonald's. With them was a suntanned man in walking shorts who looked as though he'd just walked in off a golf course.

"So there you are!" exclaimed Dad, when I appeared in the doorway. "Tom, I'd like you to meet our daughter. Apr—" He caught himself. "Valerie, this is Tom Geist from Sarasota. He's our Florida contact with the U.S. Marshals Service."

9

"The main thing you have to learn is to blend in with the scenery and avoid doing anything to attract attention," Tom told us as we sat like students in kindergarten, munching doughnuts and absorbing rules of survival. "Even your minor activities may be significant, such as three of you going together to apply for driver's licenses. There shouldn't be any problem with Valerie getting hers in Grove City, but the rest of you should take your tests somewhere else."

"You mean people notice things like that!" asked Mother.

"Small towns like this one are hotbeds of gossip," said Tom. "It's a common thing for a teenager to take a driver's test, but for a pair of adults it's more unusual. People might wonder why you've waited so long, especially since it's obvious you own a car.

"The same thing goes for getting Jason fitted for contacts. There's probably not an optometrist in Grove City, but if there is, it's better that you don't use him. We don't want word about Jason's eyes to start circulating. They're too distinctive and make him too easy to identify."

"Tell us about this man Mike Vamp," said Dad. "I don't understand how he found my family in Richmond. Max guaranteed they'd be safe there. The fact that Vamp found them anyway must mean there was a foul-up."

"Max said he can follow the scent of blood," I said. Just repeating the words was enough to make me shudder.

"That was only a figure of speech," said Tom. "The point he was trying to make was that Vamp is a pro. We've made every effort to cover your tracks to Florida. We think we've succeeded, but you can't afford to take chances. Did you leave behind any relatives in Virginia?"

"My mother," Mother said with a touch of bitterness. "Max offered her the chance to come with us, but she turned it down. I have to admit that hurts, but it doesn't surprise me. I know I was never the daughter Lorelei hoped for."

"She hasn't forgiven you your choice of a husband," said Dad. "Your parents wanted you to marry a college graduate, someone who had your social and economic background."

"It wasn't just that," said Mother. "I was always a disappointment to Lorelei. Eloping with you just put the seal on the package. She's never been able to accept that I'm not a joiner and haven't become the community leader she is. A person who spends her life putting words on paper is my mother's idea of some sort of weird recluse."

"In your current situation, that's a blessing," said Tom. "The last thing you need right now is an active social life. Choose your acquaintances carefully and don't get too close to them. For the present, at least, leave the old tenant's name on the mailbox. Have a phone installed, and I'll give you my unlisted number, but it's better that you not call me except in an emergency. Once a family is functioning under new identities, we find it's best to cut the apron strings quickly."

Before he left, he handed Dad an envelope of money. He also gave him the key to his new place of business, a fast-photo processing shop on Main Street called Zip-Pic.

That afternoon our family went shopping at Penney's. My parents tried to make it seem like a game, and Mother kept saying, "It's like being newlyweds again." We worked our way from one department to another, buying everything from silverware to bed sheets. I even talked Dad into buying me a tennis racket, since my old one had been left behind in my gym locker. Then we went to the grocery store and stocked up on food. The woman at the checkout counter asked Mother if we were new in town. Mother said yes, we had moved there from North Carolina, and asked her the best insecticide to use on roaches.

After our parents had left to drive home with our purchases, Jason and I explored the town, strolling along the sidewalks and looking in store windows. The "new" summer clothes in the stores were last year's fashions, and the picture showing at the movie theater was *Song of the South*. Jason wanted to see it, so I bought us tickets, even though I'd seen it three times back in grade school. The years hadn't stripped the lovely old film of its magic, and Jason was just as enchanted as I had been at his age. All the way home he kept squealing, "Don't throw me in the briar patch!" and hopping along beside me as though he were a rabbit. The next day we drove to Sarasota, where Jason was fitted with brown contact lenses and my parents took their drivers' tests. That afternoon I took my own test in Grove City and got a license for Valerie Weber.

Those first two days in Florida, though they couldn't have been classed as eventful, were nevertheless the activity peak of the month for us. After that life went on a downhill roll that made even our stint at the Mayflower seem exciting by comparison. I got up early each morning to play tennis with Larry, but aside from that there was nothing to do but vegetate, and in less than a week I was mired in self-pity and loneliness. Larry had to be at work by 9 A.M., and Kim had to entertain an out-of-town visitor, so the only two friends I had weren't available to do things. Mother spent her days scribbling in a notebook, while Dad spent his at Zip-Pic, going over the books and learning to run the equipment. I didn't even have my kid brother for company, for Jason made friends with two little boys down the road, and although he continued to complain about missing Chris, the three of them spent all of their time together.

Another depressing part of our life was our finances. Back home I'd never thought of our family as wealthy, since most of my classmates at Springside had comparable life-styles, but we'd lived in a comfortable home in an upper-middle-class neighborhood, and if there was something I wanted, we could usually afford it. Now Dad wasn't even able to give me an allowance. The cash supply Tom had given us hadn't been replenished, and we couldn't withdraw money from our bank in Norwood. My parents kept talking about how challenging it was to "learn to make do," as though it were some sort of game and we ought to be enjoying it. Personally, I found nothing fun about scrimping, and I hated being unable to buy the things we needed. Despite Mother's efforts to spruce up the house, she couldn't get rid of the roaches, and we didn't have a garbage disposal or a dishwasher. Worst of all, we couldn't afford a television, something I considered more a necessity than a luxury.

Three interminable weeks dragged by in that manner. Then my parents broke the monotony by having a fight. It started when Mother went down to pick up a typewriter that had turned up in a storage cabinet at Zip-Pic, and Dad told her he was too busy to bring it out to her. That typewriter had become a bone of contention between them. Every morning when Dad left for work, Mother reminded him to bring it home, and every evening he had some excuse for not having done so. First he said he had to order replacement parts for it. Then the repair shop didn't fix it right. After that he just kept "forgetting" about it, until Mother got fed up and went to get it herself.

"Too busy!" she exploded at dinner. "How could you say such a thing! Zip-Pic is hardly doing any business! This isn't a tourist town where people take vacation pictures and want them processed right away. You're lucky if you develop three rolls a day. How could you be too busy to look for the typewriter?"

"All right, so I wasn't too busy," Dad admitted. "The truth is, I was trying to postpone this very conversation. I knew that once you had access to the typewriter, you'd want to start working on your book again."

"Well, of course," said Mother. "Why shouldn't I work on my book? I can write as well in Florida as I could in Virginia. I already have the first draft written in longhand, but I can't go any further until I can type it."

"It isn't the writing itself that's the problem," Dad told her. "It's fine if you want to write for your own enjoyment. What I can't allow you to do is submit the manuscript. You can't do that without giving away where we are."

"I'll swear my editor to secrecy," Mother assured him. "I'll explain what's happened and warn him not to tell anybody."

"It will leak," Dad said. "You know that as well as I do. There are too many different departments that will need to be in touch with you. They'll be sending you galleys and copy for the jacket, and the publicity people will want to discuss promotion. There'll be no way you can keep our address secret."

"I could write the book under a pen name," Mother suggested. "Or better still, I could write it as Ellen Weber, a person who has no connection with Elizabeth Corrigan.

Later on, a new edition can be brought out under my real name."

"Stop talking like an idiot," Dad said impatiently in a tone I had never heard him use with Mother. "You've done enough reading to know how 'missing people' are located. They're usually found because they can't resist the temptation to incorporate parts of their old lives into their new lives. The bowler joins a bowling league; the bridge player joins a bridge club; the skier vacations at Crested Butte or Aspen. Do you really think you're going to bring out a book with your regular publisher, and nobody's going to catch on to who it is who wrote it? Suddenly this brand-new author surfaces who writes exactly like the missing Elizabeth Corrigan, and nobody even questions it? Come on, get real!"

"My work *makes* me real!" snapped Mother. "I've spent my whole adult life establishing myself as an author. You can't expect me to give up everything I've worked for. By the time all this is behind us and we're back home again, I'll have to start my career all over from scratch!"

Dad turned to Jason and me. "If you kids are through eating, why don't you go play cards in one of the bedrooms? Your mother and I have things we need to discuss, and I think it would be better if we did it in private."

So Jason and I went into my room and played gin rummy, while our parents continued to battle it out in the kitchen. By the following day they appeared to have reached a truce, but the air between them was chilled with icy hostility. At Mother's insistence Dad did bring home the typewriter. From that point on, she typed, just filling up paper, because, she said, it kept her from going stir-crazy. The pounding of the rusty old keys was deafening, and there was no place in the house to escape from the clatter. The noise level was increased by Jason and his cronies, who discovered trapdoors in the ceilings of all our closets and established a "secret hideout" up in the attic. They bumped and thumped around until I thought the ceiling would fall through, and by the end of the day my head felt ready to explode.

On the other hand, at night there was *too much* silence, for the road in front of our house was void of traffic, and we were not close enough to neighboring houses to have any sense of contact with other people. I would ease myself into sleep by thinking about home with the same sort of hungry longing that Dorothy felt for Kansas. I would picture our house as I had last seen it, framed by the window of Max's car, with the yard filled with flowers and my grandmother standing in the driveway. It won't be long, I would tell myself reassuringly. If there's going to be a new hearing, it will have to be soon. People can handle anything if it's temporary. By Christmas, at least, this nightmare is bound to be over.

One evening while we were at dinner the telephone rang with the first call we'd received since our phone had been installed. We all exchanged startled glances, and nobody moved.

Finally Dad nodded at Jason and said, "You get it. Your voice is the one least likely to be recognized. If it's somebody asking for 'George Corrigan,' say he has the wrong number. If he's asking for 'Philip Weber,' call me to the phone."

Jason went over and gingerly lifted the receiver.

"Hello?" he said. He paused. "You want *who*? Oh, sure." He turned to me. "It's some guy asking for *Val!*"

My heart leapt into my throat, and my mind screamed, Steve! Ridiculous as it sounds, I felt sure he had found me, spurred on by the power of love to accomplish the impossible.

I jumped up from the table and grabbed the receiver from Jason.

"Hello?" I said eagerly.

"Hi," said Larry. "How's everything going? Feel like living it up and taking in a movie?"

Disappointment descended upon me with a sickening thud.

"Thanks," I said, "but I really don't think I'll be able to. I promised my parents I'd spend the evening at home tonight." I knew I sounded ungracious, but I couldn't help it. It was one thing to have a platonic male friend to play tennis with, but another thing entirely to go out in the evening with him. I was still Steve's girlfriend even if we had to be apart for a while, and I wasn't about to cheat on him by dating someone else.

"Come on, Val," coaxed Larry. "Kim needs you more than they do. She's stuck with taking her stepsister to see *The Lost Boys* tonight. The kid's a brat, and she's driving poor Kim up the walls. I thought you and I could give her some moral support."

That threw a different light on the situation. A group of four was not the same as a twosome. Besides, with the current atmosphere at home so unpleasant, the thought of an evening away from the house was enticing.

"All right," I said. "I guess we can't let Kim down. Do you want to meet at the theater, or do you have wheels?"

"Kim's stepdad's letting her take the car," Larry told me. "The show starts at eight, so we'll pick you up around seven thirty. Where do you live? Information won't give out people's addresses."

"We're on Lemon Lane," I told him. "It's not easy to find. The house is set back in the trees and can't be seen from the road. It'll be on your right, and the mailbox in front says 'Jefferson.'"

"I know the place," said Larry. "I've been there to parties. Kim used to date Pete Jefferson before the family moved to Tampa. We'll be by for you in about half an hour."

I had not realized it was already so late. Hurriedly I excused myself from the table to take a quick shower and change from shorts into jeans. By the time I had combed my hair and applied some lipstick, Kim's car had pulled into the driveway, and its headlights were staring in through our living-room window like a pair of dragon eyes.

A moment later Larry was at the door, and Jason was racing across the room to open it.

"Hi!" he said. "Are you my sister's new boyfriend?"

"Jason!" I gasped in horror, but Larry looked pleased.

"Not yet," he said, "but it might be something worth considering."

"Mother—Dad—this is Larry Bushnell," I said quickly in an effort to ward off further remarks from my brother. "Larry's the friend I play tennis with every morning."

"It's nice to meet you," said Dad, extending his hand.

Mother said, "We're so glad Valerie's found another tennis buff. From what she says, you must be an excellent player."

"She's pretty good herself, for a girl," said Larry. "The coach at school's going to flip when he sees her serve. Tennis is a big deal here in Grove City. With Val on the team, I bet our girls make it to Nationals."

He and my parents chatted a few minutes longer, and then Kim beeped her horn to tell us to get a move on.

"Your folks seem cool," Larry said as we descended the steps and crossed the weed-infested yard to the car. "And your brother—when I first saw him, I couldn't believe it. I've never seen a kid with different-color eyes before."

The realization struck me like a fist in the stomach. Jason had not been wearing his contacts!

"Don't mention his eyes to anyone," I said hastily. "He's self-conscious about them and usually wears contact lenses."

"Whatever you say," said Larry. "I thought they looked classy." He opened the door of the car, and the dome light popped on.

"Hi, Val," said Kim. "I'd like you to meet my stepsister. Abby, this is a friend of ours, Val Weber."

The girl who was seated beside her turned to peer back at me, and a second punch in the stomach all but finished me.

"Why do you call her that?" asked Abby Keller. "That girl isn't named Val Weber, she's April Gross."

10

Of course, I did what I had to do—I bluffed. I stared at the girl as though I had never seen her before and asked in feigned bewilderment, "What are you talking about?"

She returned my stare with narrowed blue eyes, not in the least intimidated by my reaction.

"Gross," she said. "You're the girl with the 'gross' last name."

"Abby, please, don't be rude to my friends," said Kim. "How would you feel if somebody said that about *your* name?"

"That's not what I meant," said Abby. "*She* knows what I meant. She sat with me on the plane coming down from Richmond. She told me her name was April Gross and that she and her mother were going to Sarasota. Why is she pretending to be somebody else?"

"You're mistaken," I said firmly. "You may have sat next to somebody who looked like me, but my name is Valerie Weber. I've never been to Virginia, and I'm certainly not staying in Sarasota. My parents and brother and I are from North Carolina."

"That's not true!" Abby insisted. "I always remember people. I never make mistakes about things like that."

"Anybody can make a mistake," said Larry. I could tell he was having to struggle to control his temper. He motioned me into the back and climbed in after me. "Come on, Kim, let's get moving or we'll miss the start of the show. You know the line's always eight miles long on dollar night."

That statement proved to be only slightly exaggerated. When we arrived at the theater there were at least two dozen customers lined up in front of the ticket window, and by the time Kim had parked the car and we had walked back across the width of the parking lot, the line had almost doubled in length. Most of the people attending the movie were teenagers, and almost all of them seemed to know Kim and Larry. In a few minutes' time I was introduced to Sandi and Heidi and Erby and Fran and Amy and Scott and Jennifer and finally started losing track of names. The girls in particular looked me over with interest, and the one named Sandi acknowledged the introduction in such a chilly manner that I was sure she had more than a casual interest in Larry.

When we finally reached the ticket window, Larry paid for both of us, and in the lobby he insisted on buying us both popcorn. Then, since Kim and Abby had bypassed the refreshment counter and been swept along with the crowd into the theater ahead of us, we ended up finding seats several rows behind them. Suddenly, without my wanting it to happen, Larry and I were not a part of a group, but a couple.

That evening was definitely not the best of my life. The theater was small and insufficiently air-conditioned, the seats were cramped and uncomfortable, and the volume of the sound track was turned up so high that my ears felt as ready to blow as overloaded speakers. Even the movie itself was a disappointment. After gazing at the screen for a couple of minutes, I realized to my dismay that the picture was about vampires. I'd had an aversion to vampire movies ever since a fourth-grade slumber party when I'd become hysterical with terror watching *Salem's Lot.*

I would have liked to get up and walk out, but I was trapped. In the process of having my ticket and popcorn paid for, I inadvertently had become Larry's date. He made that very clear when, as a coven of greasy-haired bloodsuckers came zooming across the screen on high-powered motorcycles, his arm went snaking along the back of my seat and then slid down to settle around my shoulders.

There was something about the gesture that was so possessive that I felt like leaning forward and dumping the arm off me. It was as though he were staking a claim, and with such self-confidence that he didn't even glance over to gauge my reaction. I didn't want to blow the thing out of proportion, so for about ten minutes I sat there under the weight of the intrusive arm, munching popcorn I hadn't wanted in the first place, watching a movie I hated, and feeling miserable. Finally, when Larry's fingers started sensually massaging my upper arm, I whispered that I needed to find a rest room and hurried up the aisle and out into the lobby.

Once I had gotten that far I was tempted to keep on going. Our house was within walking distance of the theater, and the thought of being outside in the soft air of evening was enough to destroy the best of my good intentions. So strong was my desire to escape that I actually had my hand on the exit door and was trying to think of an excuse to offer later for my rudeness, when I looked out through the glass, past the light that spilled down from the marquee, and saw that rain was coming down in such a deluge that I couldn't even see past the curb to the street.

Well, so much for that, I thought, I'm here for the evening. I stood for a while, gazing out at the torrent of water crashing down from above like Niagara Falls. Finally, in an effort to further postpone my return to my seat, I went back across the lobby to the ladies' room.

There was nobody else in the rest room when I entered it, but as soon as I had stepped into one of the stalls, I heard the sound of the door to the lobby bang open and a sudden shrill burst of animated voices.

". . . supposed to be a tennis whiz," a girl was saying. "Kim says that's the whole attraction, but I don't believe it. We're sitting right behind them, and from the way he's hanging all over her, tennis is the last thing he's got on his mind."

"Kim's so naive she still believes in Santa Claus!" a second girl responded with a giggle. "Since when does her macho cousin pick girls for their muscles? Besides, she doesn't look all that athletic to me. I bet she doesn't even go out for the team."

The doors to the cubicles on either side slammed shut, but the fact that the girls could no longer see each other did nothing to decrease the babble of conversation. They simply raised their voices and continued to gossip unselfconsciously as though oblivious to the fact that the center stall was occupied.

"Did you notice she's strutting around in Guess jeans? Where do you suppose she got those, a second-hand store? Everybody can see the family's dirt poor. Her dad drives an old beat-up Plymouth and works at Zip-Pic, and my aunt, who's a checker at the store where her mother buys groceries, says she gets all the cheapest brands of everything. If they're that hard up, you wonder why the woman isn't working."

"Maybe she didn't finish high school or something."

"You don't have to have a diploma to work in the Groves. What is there about that girl that's got Lover Boy drooling? It certainly can't be the hair style. She looks like she was attacked with a pair of garden shears."

"She's somebody new in town, and our Larry likes a challenge. Sandi's problem is she makes everything too easy for him. He knows whenever he calls, she'll be sitting by the telephone."

Again the doors to the cubicles slammed simultaneously and a moment later I heard the sound of running water. The girls continued to chatter as they repaired their makeup, hashing over poor Sandi's dilemma and making more speculations about Larry's "new conquest." I considered embarrassing them by stepping out of the stall but decided I was the one who would suffer if I did. It was going to be hard enough to start a strange school in my senior year without deliberately antagonizing my new classmates.

So I stayed holed up in my ridiculous hiding place until the two of them had finished making themselves beautiful. When they left, I emerged from the stall and washed my hands at the sink, so outraged by their gossip I was shaking all over. I longed to run after them, shouting, "We are *not* poor! Back home we have a lovely home and two new model cars! My mother's an author, and my father used to work for an airline! Not only are we just as good as you are, we're a whole lot better!" The frustration I felt at not being able to stand up for myself was so intense, it was making me literally nauseated. At least there was one nasty statement I'd be able to disprove—"She doesn't look all that athletic . . . she won't go out for the team." No matter how disdainful the kids in Grove City might be of my family, they would have to stand up and take notice when they saw me on the tennis court.

As I rinsed my hands at the sink, I averted my eyes so I wouldn't have to look at myself in the mirror. It came as a shock every time I caught sight of my hair. Since arriving in Florida I'd had it evened at a beauty parlor, so it wasn't quite as dreadful as it had been originally, but instead of Rapunzel, the Princess in the Tower, the short-cropped style made me look like Peter Pan.

I rinsed my hands and thrust them under the air dryer.
Then, accepting the fact that I couldn't forestall the inevitable indefinitely, I returned to *The Lost Boys* and to Larry.

"What took you so long?" he whispered as I slid into my
seat. "You missed a lot of good stuff. The vampires fed that
kid some blood, and now he's a vampire too. He just finished trying to murder his brother in the bathtub, but that
didn't work, because the brother's dog attacked him. Now
he's outside the window, scratching on the glass, trying to
get somebody to let him in."

I gave a spontaneous shudder, which Larry misinter-
preted.

"It *is* pretty cold in here with the air-conditioning so
high."

"I'm not cold at all," I whispered, to no avail. Larry's
arm came plunging down onto my shoulders as though it
had been hanging suspended the whole time I was gone, and
there it remained like a lump of living lead until the last
vampire had been burned to a crisp, rammed through with a
spike, or both.

It was after ten by the time the movie was over. When we
left the theater it was no longer raining. There were puddles
on the sidewalk and the street was filled with water, but the
sky was clear and lighted by a pale, young moon.

"An hour ago it was pouring," I commented in surprise.

"That's how Florida is in the summertime," said Kim.
"There's not a cloud in the sky, and a few minutes later,
rain's coming down by the bucketful. Summer storms don't
usually last very long here, but while they do, they're tor-
rential."

"Was it different back in Virginia?" Abby asked slyly.

"Like I said before, I've never been in Virginia," I told
her.

I was grateful the drive to our house was not a long one.
Even though Larry didn't try to put any moves on me in the
car, I was uncomfortably aware of his presence in the seat

beside me and the fact that our relationship had been subtly altered. Even worse was being enclosed with Abby. Having her turn out to be Kim's stepsister was the sort of ironic coincidence that I would have dubbed impossible if I'd seen it in a movie. I vowed that I'd never again disclose *anything* to *anybody*. You never knew when your words would come back to haunt you. The impossible *did* sometimes happen, and Abby was proof of that.

By the time we turned onto Lemon Lane, the ditch at the side of the road had become a fast-flowing river, churning white with foam. It poured through the culverts that ran under the driveways leading back to unseen houses and emerged as wild sprays of froth, leaping high in the moonlight like demented ghosts. Kim pulled the car carefully into our driveway and around the bend between the high banks of bushes, bringing it to a stop in front of the house. Back in this pocket of shadows, trees shut off the light from the sky as effectively as the undergrowth cut off the sight of the road. Darkness lay dense and heavy on either side of us, but the beam of Kim's headlights cut a path to the porch, and lights could be seen behind the living room windows.

"Don't bother to get out," I told Larry as he reached for the door handle. "It's only a couple of yards, and I can see fine. Thanks for the movie and popcorn, and thanks for the ride, Kim."

"We were glad to have you," said Kim. "Abby's a movie freak, so I guess we'll be seeing a lot of them this summer."

I opened the door, and the dome light snapped back on. Abby had turned in her seat and was staring back at me with her sharp, blue eyes both knowing and filled with questions.

"The only movies they ever get here are old ones," she said deliberately, in the exact same tone she had used when she made that statement on the plane. "They're all so old they're already out as videos. But April—I mean Valerie— knows that already."

"We *all* know that already," Larry said irritably. "As far as we're concerned though, they're first-run here." He turned to me. "Would you like to go to the beach tomorrow? Grove City's a refueling stop for cross-state buses, so transportation to Sarasota's no problem."

"I don't think my folks would go for that," I told him. "They're into doing family things on the weekends." I wasn't sure what I wanted to do about Larry. I had no desire for our personal relationship to accelerate. On the other hand, our tennis games were so important to me that I didn't want to do anything to jeopardize them.

"Try to convince them," he said. "I'll call you in the morning."

"Fine," I told him, grateful to be spared a decision right then. "Goodnight, everybody, and thanks again for everything."

When I entered the house I knew at once that Dad and Mother had been arguing again. There wasn't a fight in progress—they both had their noses buried in books—but the air was thick with echoes of voices recently raised in anger and of unpleasant statements and shrill-toned accusations. I stood in the doorway, thinking how strange it was to see my parents seated one at each end of the sofa in a room filled with silence. Perhaps it was the harshness of the overhead light, but they both appeared older to me than they had back in Norwood. Dad's face had always been gentle and remarkably boyish, making his receding hairline seem a comical afterthought. Now, however, there was a haggard look to his features, and frown lines made shadowed trenches at the corners of his mouth. Mother looked tired and glassy-eyed and spacey, and was sipping from her everpresent glass of orange juice.

It was apparent they were waiting up for me, because as soon as I came in they both laid aside their books.

Mother spoke first, enunciating carefully, as though she were afraid her tongue would become tangled. "Your father has something he wants to discuss with you. I don't agree with his reasoning, but it seems my opinions don't count for much anymore."

"What is it?" I asked nervously, social problems forgotten.

"Larry said something this evening that bothered me," said Dad. "I gave Tom Geist a call to get his reaction to it, and he thinks—and I agree with him—that it would be better if you didn't go out for the tennis team when school starts."

"Not go out for the tennis team?" I exclaimed. "I don't understand. Why shouldn't I play tennis?"

"I didn't say you can't *play*," Dad assured me hastily. "Just don't play competitively. If you do, you'll rank high at the tournaments, and that could be dangerous."

"You don't want me to play because I'm *too good?*"

"Larry said tennis is a major sport here," said Dad. "That means the players get featured in the newspaper. As good as you are, you're a shoo-in to make it to State and, for all we know, maybe to Nationals as well. The last thing our family needs is national publicity."

"Nobody's going to recognize 'Val Weber,' " I protested. "Isn't that the whole reason we changed our names?"

"This Vamp guy knows a lot about us," said Dad. "He's sure to have been supplied with all pertinent information. He won't recognize your name, but he'll recognize *you.* He'll know I have a daughter who plays championship tennis. He'll know your age, what grade you're in, and what you look like. We can't stop people from taking pictures at meets, and we can't stop a newspaper from publishing one on the sports page."

"My tennis ability is all I have going for me here! Are you telling me all I can do is bop a ball around?" I was trying to keep my voice under control, but it seemed to be getting louder on its own accord, as if some invisible hand were turning up the volume. I whirled upon Mother. "Are you going to let him do this!"

"As I already said, my opinions don't seem to matter. Your father's decided we all have to give up everything." Mother got up from the sofa and headed unsteadily for the kitchen, trailing her fingers lightly along the wall. "I'm going to get myself another glass of orange juice."

"No, you're not," Dad told her sharply. "You've had enough. Come back here and sit down so we can discuss this."

"There's nothing left to discuss," Mother shot back at him. "You and Tom make the rules, and the rest of us follow them. I gave up my career, and April will give up tennis, but you can't expect either one of us to be happy about it."

"Our daughter's name isn't April, it's *Valerie,*" said Dad. "We can't afford to make slips like that, even when we're alone. In a town this size, everybody overhears everything. It doesn't take much to make small-town people suspicious."

That was the point when I should have told him about Abby and that Larry had seen my brother without his contacts. At that moment, however, I was too angry to trust myself to speak. I turned on my heel and, leaving my parents to finish their battle in private, went into my bedroom and shut the door behind me.

11

That night I cried myself to sleep, but once I let go of consciousness I slept like a drugged thing, too emotionally exhausted even to dream. When I awoke, it was not of my own volition but because there was somebody shaking me by the shoulder. I reluctantly opened my eyes to find my father standing by my bed in a room that was just beginning to take on form in the pale pink glow of dawn.

"Wake up," Dad said. "We've got a big day ahead of us. Your mother and I have decided it's time for a mini-vay."

"You've *what*?" It was the last thing I had expected. I made no effort to keep the contempt from my voice. "What kind of mini-vay can we have in Grove City?"

"The best," Dad said. "Disney World and Epcot Center. It's a two-hour drive, so if we want to spend a full day there, we need to get started."

"I don't feel like driving two hours to meet Mickey Mouse," I said. "The rest of you do what you want, but I'm staying here."

"Look, I know you're disappointed about the tennis,"

said Dad. "Still, sulking won't change things. If I could, I'd go back and reshuffle the cards, but I can't, so we're stuck with playing the crummy hand I've dealt us."

"How could you have gotten us into this mess?" I demanded.

"I've asked myself that a million times," Dad said quietly. "I'd like to think I was being a responsible citizen. That's what I've tried to tell myself for the past twelve months. The real truth is, I wanted to be a hero. As a kid I was one of those wimps other kids beat up on, and I only survived my teens because Max looked out for me. I was grateful for that, but it didn't do much for my ego. I met your mother when I was working at a shop at a ski resort, and she was there on vacation with her college roommate. Her friend was into partying, and your mother wasn't, so she started hanging out with me in the evenings. We fell in love, and I talked her into eloping. When her parents found out what we'd done, they nearly disowned her."

"But wasn't it Grandpa Clyde who got you your job?" I asked.

"Yes, he eventually rallied round and took care of us. Clyde didn't want his daughter married to a ski bum, and he had some sort of connections at Southern Skyways. Later he pulled some strings to have me made manager, and he and Lorelei bought us our home in Norwood. Then, out of the blue, your mother's career took off like a skyrocket, and I was left riding along on everybody's coattails. When Max came up with this chance for me to achieve something—". He paused. "I don't know why I'm bothering to explain this. The bottom line is that I wound up doing something stupid. That can't be changed, so we've just got to make the best of it."

"Talking mice aren't my idea of fun," I said.

"What is, then?" Dad asked patiently. "I'm willing to negotiate. Where would you rather go? Cypress Gardens isn't far. Or we could drive over to the beach at Sarasota."

He was trying so hard to please me that I felt guilty. I was struck by the sudden memory of a playful man with a gentle face, who had held me on his lap and told me stories at bedtime. If he saw I was becoming frightened by the violent parts, he would change the endings so everything came out as I wanted, with the three little pigs and the wolf eating dinner together and the Billy Goats Gruff playing games with the troll in the pasture. In other areas of life, however, he was powerless. There was no way he could alter our real-life story.

"I guess Disney World might be fun at that," I said softly, ashamed of myself for my earlier reaction. "Who are you going to get to run things at Zip-Pic?"

"Nobody, and I'm not going to worry about it," Dad told me. "Nobody left any film for processing yesterday. It's little wonder the business was up for grabs; the previous owner probably died of starvation. But not to worry, the program will continue to take care of us. Tom Geist drove over last night and brought us more money."

He left the room, and I got out of bed and got dressed. Then, after a hurried breakfast, we set off for Disney World.

When we first got into the car we were like a troupe of actors playing the parts of a family on a carefree vacation trip. It was obvious my parents had talked things over and made a studied decision to make the excursion a happy one. They both seemed chipper and cheerful, chatting amicably as we drove, and appeared to be looking forward to the day's activities. Jason, who had not been awake to witness the scene the evening before, must somehow have absorbed the vibes that preceded it, for he seemed bewildered by the change in the emotional atmosphere and kept glancing back and forth between Dad and Mother as though he was trying to figure out what was different about them. Soon, though, he appeared to relax and accept the situation at face value, and before a half hour had passed he was bouncing up and

down on the seat, asking every mile or two if we were almost there yet.

In an effort to calm him down, Mother suggested we play
word games, so we played Twenty Questions and Ghost and
a game where you try to find all the letters of the alphabet
on road signs. The closer we got to Orlando, the more signs
there were, and before we had reached the outskirts of the
city we had even managed to find the elusive q on a bill-
board that advertised a motel with queen-size beds.

The game had just ended with the z in La-Z-Boy Furniture when we passed a hedge shaped like the Seven Dwarfs
on parade, and Dad started singing "Whistle While You
Work." After a moment Mother began to sing with him, her
soft, sweet voice blending easily with his strong one. It had
been so long since I'd heard my parents sing together that I
had forgotten how good they could sound when they har-
monized.

They finished one Disney song and went on to another,
extending the medley to include "Someday My Prince Will
Come" and "When You Wish Upon a Star." Then they did
a rendition of "It's a Small, Small World," and Jason and I
joined in on the chorus. After that we sang the Mickey
Mouse Club song, with Jason inserting "See you real soon?
Why? Because I *like* you!" in appropriate spots. We continued getting louder and more rambunctious until by the time
we pulled into the parking area outside the gigantic amuse-
ment park we had become what we had started out by only
pretending to be, a lighthearted family having a wonderful
time together.

"There it is! There's Disney World, just like on television!" Jason cried ecstatically as the golden spires of Cinder-
ella's castle came into view. When he caught sight of a huge
Donald Duck ambling along with a cluster of balloons in its
hand, it was all I could do to restrain him from throwing
open the car door and setting out at a run across the parking lot.

Despite my initial reservations about a world filled with animated creatures, the Enchanted Kingdom did, indeed, turn out to be enchanting. When we stepped through the magical gates, dreams became reality and reality, dreams, and all the stress of the past few months evaporated. The Pirates of the Caribbean fired their cannons with gusto, but no one was hurt; ghosts danced in the spooky ballroom of the Haunted Mansion, but no one was frightened. My parents and brother and I worked our way from Frontier Land all the way to Tomorrow Land, humming along with singing bears, cruising a river on Tom Sawyer's raft, gliding beneath the ocean in a miniature submarine, all of us acting like children on a holiday.

It was almost two when we finally sat down to lunch at a table overlooking a swan-studded lake and began to discuss how to spend the remainder of the day.

"What do you say we go over to Epcot?" Dad suggested. "We can spend the afternoon looking at the exhibits there and then have dinner at one of the foreign restaurants."

"We can't leave yet! We only just got here!" cried Jason. "I haven't even been on the Jungle Cruise!"

"Your mother wants to see the 3-D movie," said Dad. "You'll like that, son, it's supposed to contain some incredible effects. Epcot should be a great educational experience."

"I don't want to get educated!" Jason insisted stubbornly. "I want to go on a boat and ride in a teacup."

"I'll stay and keep an eye on him," I offered, mellowed out by all the morning activity. "Why don't the two of you go on to Epcot? You haven't done anything alone together in ages."

"Are you sure you want to do that?" asked Mother. "There are so many things to see there, it seems dreadful to come all this distance only to miss them."

"Let the kids stay here if they want to," Dad said easily. "It's not as though we'll never be coming back. The point of the day is for all of us to enjoy ourselves, and if Jason's idea

of joy is to make himself sick in a spinning teacup, so be it."
He turned to me. "Let's meet at the gate at six. Then we'll
stop somewhere for dinner before we head home."

Predictably, the instant our parents were out of sight and
earshot, Jason burst into a spell of hyperactivity, jumping
around like a frenzied cricket and demanding to go on all
the rides Mother had forbidden because she considered
them too stimulating. He also somehow managed to take
out his contacts. One minute he was Jason, with two brown
eyes—the next, he was Bram, with one brown eye and one
green one.

"Go into the rest room and put those back in," I told
him. "You know you're not supposed to keep taking them
out. You weren't wearing them when Larry came over last
night, and he noticed your eyes and commented on them."

"I hate wearing contacts," Jason whimpered pathetically.
"How can I have a good time if my eyes feel cruddy?"

We finally agreed on a compromise, and I bought him
Mickey Mouse sunglasses, which he promised to wear until
we were back in the car. With those in place, he went dashing off like a small tornado, and from that moment on my
time was devoted to following him from one wild ride to
another and wishing that it was possible to keep him on a
leash.

The afternoon crowds were heavier than those in the
morning, and the heat of the day kept increasing as the
hours passed. By late afternoon I gladly would have settled
myself on a bench by the lake and remained there, people-
watching, until time to meet our parents. That was impossible, of course, with a pint-sized dynamo to keep track of, so
I trotted along in the churning wake of my brother, wondering how I could have been crazy enough to have volun-
teered to be his keeper.

I was standing wearily at the foot of one of the rides,
sipping a Coke and watching Jason whirl dizzily around in
a teacup, when suddenly I heard someone call out "April?"

Instinctively I started to turn in the direction of the voice, and then got a grip on my reflexes and held myself rigid. It had to be a coincidence, I assured myself, struggling to still the pounding of my heart. April is not a common name, but it isn't unique. In a complex the size of Disney World, overflowing with summer visitors, it would have been strange if there hadn't been more than one April.

That comforting thought was dispelled when the voice called "April?" once again, and then, to my utter horror, "April Corrigan?"

Hearing the name in its entirety was so unexpected that for a moment the shock of it nailed me to the ground. Then self-preservation took over, and with a hasty glance to reassure myself that Jason was safe in his cup and still wearing his glasses, I began to walk rapidly away from the Alice in Wonderland ride as though I had just remembered important business elsewhere.

"April! April, wait up! April, it's Jodi!"

The voice clicked into place, suddenly dreadfully familiar. I increased my pace until I was almost running, ducking and dodging, plowing a path through the crowd, shoving my way past people standing in line to get into Space Mountain, and nearly knocking over an elderly woman with a white-tipped cane who had not been able to see me rushing toward her. For a moment I thought the blind woman would be my salvation, for she started thrusting the cane out defensively, first on one side and then on the other, inadvertently blocking the path of the people behind me. Ironically, then, I found that my own path was blocked as well, for a gigantic Pluto, surrounded by a circle of children, seemed to materialize out of nowhere, taking up not only the walkway directly in front of me, but enough space on either side so I was stopped in my tracks.

"April!" The voice was upon me now, and a hand clamped down on my arm. "April, didn't you hear me? I've been screaming my lungs out! I was sure it had to be you the moment I saw you, even from the back with that new short haircut!"

Reluctantly, I allowed myself to be spun around and embraced by my tennis partner, Jodi Simmons.

So much had changed in my life in the weeks since I'd seen her that it startled me to find her exactly as she'd always been. Her eyes were bright with pleasure at having found me, and her nice, wide mouth looked as though it would never stop smiling. In contrast I suddenly felt a million years old, the last person on earth who belonged in Happily-Ever-After Land.

"I just can't believe this!" cried Jodi. "It's so great to see you! Are you here by yourself? April, what are you *doing* here?"

"The same thing you are," I told her, keeping my tone light. "I'm pretending to be ten years old again. This has to be the most fabulous place in the world."

"I can't believe it!" Jodi repeated, continuing to cling to my arm as though she were afraid I would disappear if she let go of me. "The last thing I ever expected was to run into *you* here! Do you have any idea how worried we've all been? Sherry said you were called to the counselor's office, and from that point on no one ever saw you again!"

"My parents decided they needed a vacation," I said. Even to my ears the statement sounded ridiculous.

Apparently it had the same effect upon Jodi, for she raised one eyebrow in an expression of disbelief.

"Oh, come on!" she exclaimed. "Who do you think you're kidding? Nobody goes on vacation two weeks before finals! Even your grandmother doesn't know where you are. I stopped by her condo one day to drop off your tennis racket, and she told me she didn't even have an address to ship it to."

"There's a reason for that," I said, "but I'm not free to talk about it. How is everything back home? Did the tennis team do well in the state competition?"

"State was a disaster," said Jodi. "Since you weren't there, I had to play with Cynthia, and you know what a dud she is at the net. We lost the first round of doubles, and that threw my game off so badly that I ended up not making it to finals in singles either. But enough about me, I want to know about *you*. You'll be back before school starts, won't you?"

"No, but I'll be there for the second semester," I said. "Tell Coach Malloy to hold a place for me on the team. Look, Jodi, it's been wonderful seeing you, but I've got to split. I'm supposed to be meeting my brother at the Haunted Mansion."

"But you can't run off without filling me in on what happened!" Jodi protested. "Everybody's going to freak out when I tell them I saw you. It's been like you just disappeared off the face of the earth! I saw Sherry and Steve at Ashley Steinmetz's pool party last weekend, and they said neither one of them had heard one word from you. There are all sorts of far-out rumors going around, like you had to move because your dad testified in that drug case."

"Sherry and Steve were at the Ashley's party together?" I asked her. "You don't mean—you *can't* mean—the two of them are dating!"

"Oh, just off and on," said Jodi, obviously embarrassed. "You know how it is with guys when their girlfriends take off somewhere. I'm sure it doesn't mean anything, so don't let it bother you. Steve will be leaving for college in a few weeks anyway, and of course you'll be back to go to the Christmas parties with him."

"Of course," I said. "I wouldn't miss the bash at Sherry's house, I had such a wonderful time at that party last year."

Without further comment, I jerked my sleeve from her fingers and set off at a run in the direction of the Haunted Mansion. I must have crashed into a dozen people on my headlong flight into nowhere, for I carried no cane to warn them I was blinded by tears.

12

My parents could tell I'd been crying when we met at the gate. When I told them about meeting Jodi, they both turned pale, and the carefree mood of the day was quickly dissipated.

Immediately, Dad asked me, "What did you tell her?"

"Nothing," I said defensively. "I didn't tell her anything."

"You must have said *something*! You couldn't have stood there in silence. Didn't she even ask you where we're living?"

"Of course, but I didn't give anything away," I said. "I didn't even say we were living in Florida. I told her we were vacationing at Disney World. For all she knows we could have flown in from Alaska."

"It sounds as though you handled it well," said Mother.

"This was all my fault," said Dad. "We never should have come here. I don't know what possessed me to suggest such a thing. Disney World is the biggest vacation resort on the whole East Coast. How could we *not* have run into some-body we knew here?"

"Jodi said Steve and Sherry are dating," I said miserably.

"So that's why you've been crying!" Mother put her arms around me. "I can see why you're upset, but I'm sure it doesn't mean anything. Steve is bound to be lonely and miss you, and since Sherry is your best friend, it probably makes him feel closer to you to be with her."

"There are other fish in the sea," Dad said unfeelingly. "Adolescent romance is the least of our problems."

"How can you be so insensitive!" exclaimed Mother. "It's natural for a girl to feel hurt when something like this hap-pens."

"It's time Val grew up and got her priorities in order," said Dad. "If she wants to date, there are teenage boys in Grove City."

"You're a fine one to talk about setting priorities," snapped Mother. "Where were *your* priorities when you put all our lives on hold so you could play James Bond?" By the time we were in the car, the two of them had settled into stony silence, and we drove straight back to Grove City without stopping for dinner.

The phone was ringing when we entered the house. It was Larry.

"Where have you been?" he demanded. "I've been calling all day."

"We just got back from Disney World," I told him.

"I thought we were going to the beach today," he said accusingly. "What made you decide to throw me over for Pluto?"

"I didn't," I said. "Dad sprang this trip on me this morn-ing. Besides, our plan to go to the beach wasn't definite. I told you I had to check it out with my folks."

"And *I* told *you* I'd call in the morning," said Larry. "When a girl knows I'm going to call her, I expect her to be there. I'm not a guy who appreciates being stood up."

The surliness of his voice was more than I could handle. The day had been upsetting enough without this added unpleasantness. *"I* don't appreciate being snarled at!" I exploded. When I heard him draw in a breath to fire back a retort, I did something I'd never done to anyone before—I hung up on him.

The discovery that Steve was dating Sherry was so devastating that for most of the week that followed I had no energy for anything. Without my regular tennis games to get me up and moving, I continued to lie in bed long past my usual rising time, listening to the rest of the house come to life on the far side of my bedroom walls. If I blocked everything else from my mind and concentrated on the surface of the wall across from me, the mapwork of cracks in the plaster looked like a spider web, and I found that if I stared at it long enough, I could even make out the shape of a fly ensnared in it. Gazing up at the ceiling was just as depressing. Rain had leaked through the roof to form puddles in the attic, and the stain on the plaster above me grew larger with each rainfall. It had spread so far that a portion was over my bed, and I kept expecting something dark and nasty to leak down on me. My bedroom became a symbol of our life in Grove City, and by the time I dragged myself out to face what was left of the morning, I was so immersed in self-pity that I had no desire to go anywhere or do anything.

It was Kim who jolted me to life and started me functioning again. Four days after the Disney World trip, she phoned me.

"I just thought I'd call and check in with you," she said awkwardly. "Larry's plenty freaked out about your breakup."

"Our breakup?" I exclaimed. "What do you mean, our breakup? You can't break up with somebody unless you've been dating. All Larry and I had going between us were tennis balls."

"That's not the way he wanted it, though," Kim told me.

"He thinks you're cool, and he was planning to start going out with you. You've got to understand how it is with Larry. He's used to having the local girls fall all over him, and he takes it as a put-down when somebody doesn't."

"Poor baby," I said sarcastically. "Did he ask you to tell me that?"

"Not exactly," said Kim, "but he did hint around about it. What he wants me to do is find out if you're still pissed off at him or whether, if he was to call you, you'd want to start seeing him again."

"Maybe if he apologized—"

"That's not his style. Larry never apologizes to anybody for anything."

The day was hot, and it hadn't rained for a week, so I knew the courts at the school would be dry and hard. Dad was at Zip-Pic, Mother was busy at the typewriter, and Jason and his friends were holed up in their hideout, thumping around in the attic like a herd of elephants. My muscles felt tight from lack of exercise, and the thought of a game of tennis was irresistible.

"Tell him to call me," I said. "I shouldn't have hung up on him. I was feeling rotten that evening and overreacted." Princess April would never have made such a statement, but Valerie Weber was desperate with loneliness and boredom.

Either Kim called Larry immediately, or he'd been standing there at her elbow when she made her call to me, because less than five minutes later he was on the phone. As Kim had predicted, he didn't apologize, which irritated me so much that I didn't either. Neither of us referred to the last conversation we'd had, we just made a date to play tennis at seven the next morning. After that we swung naturally back into our old routine, and our daily morning tennis games became the norm again. We also started playing in the early evening after the sun had dropped below the treeline and the blazing afternoon heat had lifted from the courts.

One evening, after playing three sets at twilight, we stopped for Cokes at McDonald's and found ourselves in line behind Fran and Amy, two of the girls I'd met at the vampire movie. I was worried at first that they might be the girls from the rest room, but as soon as we started talking, I knew that their voices weren't the ones that I'd heard there. We ended up sharing a table, and in the course of conversation, Amy invited us to a party she was having on Saturday.

I realized the invitation was directed primarily at Larry, but he turned to me and asked, "Are you busy that night?" When I said no, he flashed me that cocky grin of his. "Great," he said. "I'll pick you up around eight, then."

So once again I was committed to a formal date with him. This time, though, I didn't feel guilty about it. Steve wasn't sitting at home by himself every evening, and if he could date Sherry for parties, then I could date Larry. Besides, it wasn't as though this would ever get serious. There had once been a time when I'd been attracted by the burly, muscle-man type, but my taste in boys had changed since I'd started dating Steve, and Larry's gigantic ego was a definite turnoff. Still, I felt sure he'd be fun to be with at a party, and fun was something I very much needed.

I went to that party determined to have a good time. What I ended up doing instead was talking too much. I blame myself, but I also blame the punch. Amy's parents were out of town, and she and Fran and their boyfriends had created a frothy concoction they'd christened "Suicide." I woke up the following morning with a skull-splitting headache and a tongue that was stuck to the roof of my mouth with invisible Velcro.

The punch was deceptive because it tasted like fruit juice, but I have to admit I knew there was something else in it, and I drank it because I wanted to feel looser and happier. When Larry and I first got to the party I was uptight and nervous, surrounded by so many strangers who had known each other since kindergarten. To make things worse, Sandi was there, encircled by a tight group of buddies who kept glaring at me and whispering to each other and making me feel more and more uncomfortable. After two or three swallows of punch I started to feel better. Tension ran out of me the way it did after a hard game of tennis, and my artificial smile began to lose its rigidity. Then Amy put on some records, and Larry whipped me out onto the dance floor, and within a couple of minutes the room was a disco. When we finally took a break, we were both perspiring, and my heart was pounding so hard that my ears were ringing. Larry thrust another cup of "Suicide" into my hand, and I gulped down the tangy liquid gratefully.

Sometime later I found myself in the yard, half sitting, half lying on one of those aluminum chaises with plastic strips that cut into your back like a waffle iron. The marvelous thing was that Steve was there beside me. My eyes were closed, and I knew I was probably dreaming, but if I was, I had no desire to wake up. Steve's arms were tight around me, and he was kissing my face and my neck and was whispering all sorts of beautiful things in my ear.

"Baby," he whispered. "Val—" His mouth came down hard on mine, and his hands, which had worked their way inside the back of my blouse, were fumbling awkwardly around with the hooks on my bra. The lips that were pressed to mine had a foreign taste to them, and abruptly the wonderful dream gave way to reality. This wasn't the way Steve acted, and Steve didn't call me Val.

"Let go of me, Larry," I said, trying to wriggle out from under him.

"Come on, baby, don't play games with me," Larry muttered huskily. "We've seen each other almost every day for a month now. If you didn't like me, you wouldn't be spending so much time with me."

"You don't understand," I said. "I already have a boyfriend back in Virginia. I wouldn't feel right making out with somebody else."

There was a moment of silence.

Then Larry said, "*Virginia?* I heard you tell Abby you'd never even been there."

"I mean North Carolina," I said. "I've had too much punch."

Larry pulled his arms out from under my back and straightened up on the chaise to sit looking down at me. His face was hidden by shadow, but mine was raised to the sky and illuminated by moonlight, and I felt a rush of terror at what he might see there.

"I didn't mean—" I began.

"Yes, I think you *did* mean," Larry said quietly. "Abby may be a pill, but the kid's not stupid. You *did* sit next to her on the plane coming down here. She knew you were from Virginia, because you *told* her so."

"What does it matter?" I said. "Who cares where I come from? It doesn't make any difference if it's Durham or Norwood."

"The difference is that you lied about it," said Larry. "Abby said you told her your name was April. Why did you lie to Kim and me and say it was Valerie?"

"Because it *is!*" I insisted. "My name *is* Valerie! The only thing I lied about was coming from Durham!" The sour taste of punch surged up into my throat, and I swallowed hard to keep it from rising farther. "I don't feel good. Please, Larry, I want to go home."

"All right," said Larry. "But don't expect this to be the end of it. I'll take you home, but I want to know what's going on. I don't like being lied to and made a fool of."

To my relief, he didn't try to interrogate me during the drive, but once he had brought the car to a stop in our driveway, he placed his hand on my arm to keep me from getting out.

"What are you doing here in Grove City?" he asked me.

"Why did your family move here in the first place? It's not as though you had relatives here, and it certainly couldn't have been so your dad could buy Zip-Pic." He paused, and when I didn't respond, he continued. "Is your last name really Weber? I bet it isn't."

"Of course it is!" I shot back at him defiantly. "We moved here because we were having financial problems. The business my father owned back home went under, and he wanted to go somewhere else and make a fresh start."

"You mean he went bankrupt?" asked Larry.

"No, not exactly."

"Nobody comes to Grove City to seek his fortune. What's he running away from, trouble with the law? Embezzlement, maybe, or income tax evasion? A man doesn't change his name without a good reason."

"You've got everything wrong," I said angrily. "My dad's no criminal. You don't have any right to cross-examine me, and I don't have to tell you anything I don't want to." I jerked away from his hand and got out of the car. The headlights paved a straight, bright path to the porch, and I made it nearly that far before I threw up.

The next morning I was so sick I didn't get up. I let Mother think I was coming down with stomach flu and lay in bed with a pillow pressed over my eyes, cursing myself for the stupid things I had said and trying to convince myself that, since Larry, too, had been swigging down punch, he might not remember the whole of our conversation.

As the day dragged by, my hangover gradually lessened, although I couldn't believe I would ever feel good again. By midafternoon I was able to stagger to the shower, where I stood, shaky and rubber-kneed, under a pounding cascade of water and vowed I would spend the rest of my life as a teetotaler. I was able to force down some soup and toast for dinner, and by eight that night I was flat on my back in bed again, trying to read and feeling twice as drained and exhausted as I would if I'd spent the day in productive activity.

I was just getting ready to turn off the bedside lamp when there was a rap on the door and my father came in with a handful of fifty-dollar bills.

"These are yours," he said as he placed them on the bureau top. "Tom came over tonight to bring us money. He also came to tell us that Loftin was killed today."

"Loftin was killed!" I repeated in shocked bewilderment. "How can that be? I thought he was locked up in prison."

"He was released on bail when his lawyer filed for an appeal," Dad said. "According to Tom, he was mowing his lawn this morning when a car drove by and somebody leaned out and shot him. He died in the ambulance on the way to the hospital."

"I don't understand," I said. "Why would anybody kill him? It's not as though *he* had been working as a spy for the government."

"I can only guess that the dealers he serviced were afraid the appeal would go through and there would be a retrial," said Dad. "Given a second chance to turn state's evidence, Loftin might have been more receptive to the idea of plea bargaining."

"Then it's over!" The statement sounded so wonderful, I said it again. "It's over—does that mean we can go home now?"

My father didn't respond to that question directly. Instead, he said, "Loftin wasn't the one who hired Vamp. At the time Jim Peterson was killed, he was still in prison. Loftin supplied a nationwide network of dealers, and they were the ones responsible for hiring a hitman. People like that don't think twice about disposing of stool pigeons, and they're sure to consider me as great a threat as Loftin."

"But, you *aren't*," I said, and then reconsidered the statement as something I'd heard Max say leapt into my mind.

He's knocking over the first in a line of dominoes. "Could you really expose these people and testify against them?"

"No," Dad said. "I was never given their names, but the dealers have no way of knowing that, so I'm high on their hit list."

I motioned toward the pile of bills on the bureau. "What's all this for? Why are you giving me money?"

"It's reimbursement for your bedroom furniture," Dad told me. "Everything sold for a fraction of what it was worth, but I guess we ought to be grateful to end up with this much. I'm sure Max did his best with the sale of the house, but with real estate values down, we took a loss on that too."

"The house!" I exclaimed. "Max sold our house out from under us? Where are we going to live when we go back?"

"We'll play it by ear," said Dad. "We'll see how it goes. Right now we need the money more than the house. There's no way I'll ever be able to make a living from Zip-Pic, and I don't know how long the program will continue to pick up the tab for us."

"You're making it sound like we're going to be stuck here forever!" Breathlessly I waited to hear a denial. When that didn't come, I regarded him with horror. "Are you trying to tell me we're not going back *at all?*"

"We'll have to play it by ear," Dad said again.

"You made me believe we were going to be back by Christmas!"

"I never told you that. You just wanted to believe it. It's possible we may be able to go back someday. There's no way of knowing what the situation will be like a few years from now. Right now, what's important is that we're safe and together. As long as we have each other, we can get along anywhere."

"But this is the year I have to apply to Duke!"

"Duke's out," said Dad. "Too many of your classmates are going there, and they'll know you as April Corrigan, not

Valerie Weber. There's a nice little college in Sarasota called New College. I'm sure you won't have any trouble getting accepted there."

I opened my mouth to object, but he wouldn't listen.

"Don't say it," he told me brusquely. "I don't want to hear it. I've just finished having this same conversation with your mother. She's taking it hard and is putting the blame on Max. I just can't deal with another hysterical scene right now."

He left the room, and I lay there, trembling with fury and feeling as though the world had fallen out from under me. It was so unfair! I hadn't done anything to deserve this! And all this time I'd believed our exile was temporary! Dad said the important thing was the fact that our family was together and safe, but I didn't even feel that I had a family anymore. All the warmth and solidity was gone from our lives, and my parents had changed so much that I hardly knew them. The only thing in the world I wanted was to go home. There had to be some way out of this nightmare!

13

I awoke the next morning knowing what I was going to do. It was as if somehow during the night the plan had materialized of its own accord. I'd known Mother to say that at times that happened to her when she was having a difficult time with one of her novels. She would go to bed with the problem churning in her brain and when she woke up in the morning she would know instinctively how to solve it.

That was how it was with me that morning in August when I awoke to see the money lying on the bureau. Despite its having sold for less than it was worth, I knew the antique furniture had been valuable. Now, when I counted the money, I found there was over four hundred dollars, far more than I needed for a one-way plane ticket to Norwood.

My preference, of course, would have been to approach my parents directly and tell them I wanted to go home and live with my grandmother. I knew, though, this was something they would not sanction. From what Dad had said, he was determined to keep us together no matter how miserable the circumstances, and Mother, for her part, would not

want me living with Lorelei, even if it were just for my final
year of high school. She and her mother had different opinions about everything. Mother thought Lorelei's life-style
was superficial and shallow, while Lorelei couldn't understand why Mother was so reclusive. My mother had always
felt threatened by my closeness to my grandmother, as
though she were afraid her value system might rub off on
me.

So, although I would have liked to have acted more hon-
orably, I knew I would have to put my plan into effect
without my parents' consent and trust that they loved me
enough to understand and forgive me.

I lay in bed for an hour, working out the details, as the
early morning sunlight slowly lifted, moving the leaf shadows into new positions on the cracked surface of the wall
across from the window. Getting to Norwood would not be
a problem in itself. The risk was in having my parents get
wind of what I was planning and intercept me at the Sarasota Airport before my plane took off. Ideally, it would be
best if they didn't find out I had left until I was at Lorelei's
condo. I decided the best thing to do would be to set myself
up with an alibi, not just for the day I was leaving, but for
the next day as well.

I accomplished that by asking Mother if I could spend
the weekend at Kim's while her parents were visiting relatives in Miami.

"Kim doesn't want to go with them, but her folks aren't
willing to leave her at home by herself," I said.

There had been a time when I could not have lied to my
mother; in fact, I had never been comfortable lying to *anyone*. But in the past three months I had become practiced in
deception, and the words slipped out of my mouth sounding
easy and natural.

As I had expected, Mother was agreeable.

"It's nice you're finding some girlfriends here," she told

me. The second half of the statement remained unspoken—
because we're going to be here for a very long time.

The rest of the arrangements fell into place with equal
ease. Since Mother was home all day, I couldn't call the
airport from the house, so I walked to town and made plane
reservations from a pay phone. It was a relief to find fate
was working in my favor, and I was able to book a seat on a
flight on Eastern that left Sarasota the next afternoon.

That night I had a difficult time eating dinner. Despite
the scene they'd been through the previous evening, my parents were making an effort to be pleasant and communica-
tive. Somehow that made it harder than if they had been
cold to each other, because the lack of hostility reminded
me of happier times. As I sat there, listening to their familiar voices making everyday conversation, a core of loneliness twisted deep inside me, and I knew I was going to miss
my family terribly. Still, I reminded myself, it wouldn't be
forever. The time would have to come when they would
return to Virginia, and meanwhile I would know where they
were and could write to them, even though they couldn't
respond to my letters.

Although I was no longer rising at dawn to play tennis, I
was up the next morning in time to have breakfast with my
father and to give him a good-bye hug as he left for work.

He seemed pleased and surprised at the unaccustomed
display of affection. "Have a nice day, honey," he said
warmly. "I'll see you tonight."

"I'm going to be spending the weekend at Kim's," I reminded him.

"That's right, I forgot," Dad said. "Well, you girls behave
yourselves. Don't throw any wild parties just because Kim's
parents are gone." He smiled to let me know he was only
joking, and I was glad he didn't know about the past weekend.

After breakfast I went to my room and packed my overnight bag, cramming it as full as I could with clothes and

possessions. I had left a closetful of clothes behind in Norwood, but I didn't know whether or not they would still be there. It was painful to think that the lovely formal I'd never worn might have been given to Goodwill or consigned to a secondhand store, but since our house and furniture had been sold, it was possible our personal possessions had been also.

It was midmorning when I finally came into the kitchen to find Mother, as usual, seated at the table, typing.

"I thought you told Dad you wouldn't submit that," I said.

"I won't, but I have to finish it anyway," said Mother. "I can't seem to make myself stop in the middle and leave it hanging. My identity is all tied up with writing. I guess I'm not a very adaptable person." She gestured toward my suitcase. "You don't want to carry that all the way to Kim's house. Why don't you leave it for Dad to bring over later?"

"It's not heavy," I said, "and I have my tennis stuff in it. If it doesn't rain, we might want to bat some balls around."

"In the afternoon heat?" exclaimed Mother. "You kids must be crazy! At least wear a hat so you won't keel over from sunstroke."

How could I deceive somebody who trusted me so totally? For a moment I didn't think I'd be able to go through with it. Then I thought about what she'd said about needing her own identity and realized the statement applied to me as well. I was April Corrigan, Steve's girlfriend, the "princess" of Springside Academy, the star of their tennis team, a girl who was guaranteed acceptance by Duke because her mother and grandmother both had gone there. I was *not* Valerie Weber, whose hobby it was to "bat balls around," and whose only opportunity for higher education was at a school with the unlikely name of New College.

So I swallowed my guilt, kissed Mother good-bye, and left. Jason and his two friends were out in the yard, attempting to get a basketball through a hoop that Dad had attached to a beam at the front of the carport. When he saw me come out with my suitcase, he paused with the ball in his hands and regarded me with inquiring brown eyes.

"Looks like you're going on a mini-vay," he speculated.

"I'm going to spend the weekend at Kim's," I told him.

"I forgot to tell you, your boyfriend called," said Jason. "It was yesterday while you were out, and he said he'd call back."

"Larry Bushnell is *not* my boyfriend," I said firmly. "He's an egocentric creep, and I never want to see him again."

I continued on down the driveway to the point where it curved away from the trees, and then I stopped and turned to look back at the house. A boy jumped into the air and sank a basket, and I realized with a sense of shock that it was Jason. In the short time since we'd left Norwood my brother had changed. He'd lost his baby look and become taller and rangier. What would he be like the next time I saw him?

Impulsively I set down the suitcase and ran back up the length of the driveway to catch him up in a tight, fierce hug.

"What's that for?" Jason demanded in embarrassment.

"Just because," I said.

"Because why?"

"Because I *like* you!"

"That's from the Mickey Mouse Club song," he explained to his friends as he struggled manfully to squirm out of my embrace. "My sister's in a weird mood. She's not usually this goofy."

The hike into town was one I had become accustomed to, but I wasn't used to being weighed down by a suitcase. The overnight bag was heavier than I had been willing to admit to Mother, and I kept having to stop and switch it from one hand to the other to give my arms alternating rest periods. Even so, I reached the filling station on Main Street in plenty of time to intercept the cross-state bus. An hour later

I arrived at the Sarasota bus terminal, where I was able to get a taxi to the airport.

I checked in at the Eastern desk to get my seat assignment and pay for my ticket and then headed for the line of telephones along the far wall. I'd not made any out-of-state calls from Grove City for fear there might be some way they could be traced back to us. Now I found my hand shaking as I dialed Steve's number and stood waiting impatiently as the phone rang.

The voice that answered was not the one I had hoped for.

"Hello, Billy," I said. "May I speak to Steve, please?"

"He's not here right now," Steve's little brother informed me. "He's going to be back for dinner though. Is this Sherry?"

"No," I said. "This isn't Sherry, it's April."

"April?" Billy exclaimed excitedly. "Where are you calling from? Steve said you moved and he didn't know where you went."

"I did move, but I'm on my way back," I told him. "I'm getting in at the airport at six tonight, and if he can, I'd like Steve to meet my plane. Do you have something to write with so I can give you the flight number?"

"I'll go find a pencil," said Billy, dropping the receiver.

His search for a pencil seemed to take an eternity, and I had to keep depositing coins to keep the line open. Finally he was back again, and I gave him the information and had him repeat it back to me to make sure he had written it down correctly.

I pressed the hook, released it, and dialed again. This time the phone rang for such an extended period that I was beginning to think my grandmother wasn't home. This wouldn't have been surprising, since it was a Saturday afternoon, a time when she often played bridge with friends or attended some social function at the Norwood Country Club.

I was just getting ready to hang up when the phone was answered, but instead of a friendly voice there was silence.

"Hello?" I ventured tentatively. "Hello, is that Lorelei?"

"April?" My grandmother's voice sounded strained and unnatural. "Why are you calling here? Has something happened?"

It was far from the enthusiastic greeting I had expected.

"No, everything's fine," I said. "Nothing's happened to anybody."

"Then what are you calling here for?" Lorelei asked accusingly. "Even your mother isn't allowed to phone me. Whatever you do, don't tell me where you are. There's always a chance there may be a tap on the line."

"I won't tell you anything," I said, "and I'm calling from a pay phone. Lorelei, I'm coming home. I'm flying in this evening. I want to live with you until I finish high school and then go on to Duke like we always planned I would."

"That's a poor idea," said Lorelei. "What do your parents say? I can't believe your mother would let you come here."

"It's my idea, not theirs," I confessed reluctantly. "In fact, they haven't even discovered I've left yet. There's a boy, Larry Bushnell, that I play tennis with, and I've told my folks I'm spending the weekend at his cousin's house."

"Turn straight around and go back to your parents," Lorelei told me. "I don't want you coming here, and I don't want you calling again. It isn't safe. Some terrible things have happened. You probably don't know this, but Richard Loftin has been murdered."

"Dad told me," I said. "That has nothing to do with me, though. Mr. Loftin knew the identities of some drug dealers, and they were afraid his testimony was going to incriminate them. I'm not a threat to anybody, I'm just a teenager. All I want is to come home to finish high school, and after that—"

I was interrupted by the voice of the long distance operator saying my time was up and asking me to deposit more coins. Since my call to Billy Chandler had depleted my supply of change, I knew I had to end the conversation quickly.

"I *am* coming home," I said. "You can't talk me out of it. I hope you'll let me live with you, but if you won't, then maybe I can board with one of my school friends."

Without waiting for a response, I hung up the phone. I spent the rest of the time before my flight was called writing a letter to my parents. In it I explained what I was doing and told them that I loved them and was going to miss them but couldn't continue living like a criminal in hiding. I bought a stamp in the airport gift shop and dropped the envelope into a mailbox in the lobby before going out to the gate to board the plane.

On this flight I was lucky enough to have a silent seatmate. I sat next to the window, and the man next to me was dressed in a business suit and carried a briefcase. He spent the whole flight engrossed in paperwork, while I sat looking out the window at clouds that billowed beneath the plane like quilted padding on an innerspring mattress and tried to imagine my parents' reaction to my letter. If I'd timed things right, it would arrive on Monday morning at approximately the time I was expected to return from Kim's house. My mother would receive it and would phone my father. I pictured the two of them running the gamut of emotions from shock, to anger, to disappointment, and finally—I hoped—to understanding and acceptance.

The stewardess brought around dinner trays, and I took one and nibbled at the roll and ate some of the salad. My throat felt so constricted it was difficult to swallow. The closer we got to Norwood, the more keyed-up I became. Lorelei's reaction to my phone call had been an unpleasant shock to me. Her condo was plenty large enough for two people, and she had always encouraged me to come and spend the night with her. Why had she sounded so inhospitable on the telephone? Didn't she want her granddaughter back in her life again? And what about Steve, did he still consider me his girlfriend? What if I got off the plane and he wasn't there to meet me?

The stewardess came up the aisle, collecting the dinner trays, and I handed my plate of food back to her almost untouched. By the time we began our descent into the Norwood Airport, I had worked myself into such a state of apprehension that I could hardly manipulate the clasp on the seat belt.

The plane touched down and taxied up to the gate. Pulling my bag out from under the seat in front of me, I got in line with the rest of the passengers as they moved down the aisle and out into the terminal.

A handsome dark-haired boy in a red and white rugby shirt was standing at the side of the ramp.

"April!" he called. "April, I'm over here!"

"Steve!" I cried. "Oh, Steve!" and, letting my suitcase fall to the floor, I rushed to throw myself into his outstretched arms.

14

"You came!" I exclaimed, burying my face in the hollow where Steve's neck met his collarbone and inhaling the well-remembered odor of warm skin and pine-scented after-shave.

"Of course I came," he said, hugging me back. "When Billy told me you'd called, I could hardly believe it. I'd just about given up hope of ever seeing you again. When you came down that ramp, I had to look twice to recognize you. I'd never pictured Rapunzel with her beautiful hair cut off." He pushed me gently away so he could look at me. "Solve the mystery for me. Where have you been?"

"Don't ask," I said. "I'm not allowed to talk about it. We left because of Dad's testimony at the Loftin trial. A man was killed, and we had to go into hiding. It was awful, and I've very glad to be home."

"What about your family?" Steve glanced past me, over my shoulder, as though he expected to see them appear on the ramp behind me.

"I'm here alone," I said. "I'm going to live with my

grandmother. At least, I hope Lorelei's going to let me live with her. She wasn't very receptive when I told her I was coming, but I don't think she'll slam the door on me when I land on her doorstep."

"I'm sure she won't," said Steve. "She'd never do that. She was probably too surprised to know what to say. Jodi tried to call her after seeing you at Disney World, but she wasn't ever able to get in touch with her." He picked up my suitcase and, putting his other arm around me, began to walk me back through the terminal toward the lobby. "Everybody here has been worried about you. The way you left was so crazy. When you weren't at the tennis courts that afternoon, I thought we'd just gotten our wires crossed, but that night when I went to your house and found it all locked up with the car still parked in the driveway, I freaked out. That's when I realized that something serious had happened."

"It was all so fast," I said. "We weren't allowed to make phone calls. At first we thought we would only be gone a few days. The days turned into weeks, and the weeks into months. I felt as though I'd been sucked into some sort of time warp."

"I was sure, wherever you'd gone, you'd be back for the prom," Steve said. "Then, when you weren't, I thought you'd resurface for graduation. When I stepped out onto that stage to get my diploma, I kept telling myself you'd come in late and were sitting in the back."

"I wrote you I couldn't be here for that," I reminded him.

"I haven't had a word from you since you left."

His words sent my mind sliding furtively toward a dark pool of secret knowledge, and I hurriedly yanked it back onto safer ground. The fact that Steve hadn't received my letter meant nothing. It could have been lost in the mail, or the stamp might have come unglued, or the ink could have smeared so the address was illegible. Since there hadn't been any return address on the envelope, I wouldn't have gotten it back if it hadn't been delivered.

"I wrote," I said. "I'm sorry the letter didn't reach you." I paused and then asked casually, "How are things with Sherry?"

"Just fine," Steve said a little too quickly for comfort. "When Billy gave us your message, she was so excited. At first she wanted to come to the airport with me, but we decided it would be better for her to call you tomorrow."

"Sherry was with you when Billy told you I'd called?" I tried to keep it from sounding like an accusation.

"Well, yes," Steve said uncomfortably. "She'd stopped by the house. She was as happy as I was to learn you were back."

"What was she doing at your place? Had you been out together?"

"A bunch of us had a picnic over at Grant's Park," Steve said. "Rick and Traci, Debbie and Reed, Jodi and Michael—"

"In other words, it was a couples party," I said, phrasing the question as though it were a statement. "Jodi mentioned that you and Sherry were dating. It sure didn't take you long to find somebody to replace me."

"It wasn't like that at all," Steve said defensively. "Sherry and I started hanging out together because we were trying to figure out what had happened to you."

"And one thing led to another?" I asked sarcastically, pulling free of the arm he had slung around my shoulders.

"It wasn't until the For Sale sign went up in your yard that we thought you weren't coming back and we started dating." He put his hand on my arm. "Please don't be mad, April. I'm really happy you're home, and so is Sherry."

Out in the parking lot he loaded my suitcase into the backseat of his Honda and opened the door so I could climb in on the passenger's side. Then he went around and got into the driver's seat. He kept both hands on the wheel as he pulled out of the parking area and made no move to encourage me to snuggle against him. For my own part, I sat rigidly on my side of the car, too hurt and angry to try to make conversation.

"Do you want to stop for something to eat?" Steve asked awkwardly.

"No, I'd like to go straight to Lorelei's," I told him. "I need to find out if she's going to let me stay there."

"If there's any problem, I'm sure you can sleep at Sherry's," Steve said. "No matter what you may think, she's still your friend."

"With a friend like that, I don't need any enemies," I said bitterly. "If I can't spend the night at Lorelei's, I'll crash at Jodi's."

The Golden Ridge Condominiums, where Lorelei had moved after my grandfather died, were a group of colonial-style town houses enclosed by a wrought-iron fence. The security guard was a friendly black man named Pat whom I had come to know well during the five years Lorelei lived there. Now, as Steve brought the car to a stop at the gate, I leaned across him so Pat could see who I was.

"Hi!" I called. "It's me. I'm here to see my grandmother."

I expected him to immediately raise the gate for us, but instead he came out of the guardhouse, gave Steve a long, hard stare, and walked all the way around the car, looking in windows.

He stopped when he came abreast of the window on my side.

"Your grandmother didn't leave word she was expecting company," he said. "I'll have to call for permission to let you through."

"Pat, you've known me since I was twelve!" I exclaimed. "Since when do I have to have special permission to visit here?"

"Things are different now," Pat said. "The manager's

clamped down. We don't let people in anymore unless their names are on a guest list. Your grandmother doesn't have anybody's name on her list. She wants me to call and check about every visitor."

"I can't believe that," I said. "It's not at all like her."

"Like I said, things are different now," Pat repeated patiently.

He went back into the gate house, and through the glass of the security room window I could see him dialing the phone. He spoke briefly, hung up, and came back out.

"She said I can let you in, but nobody else," he said. "She doesn't want you to bring your friend in with you."

"Maybe she's in her nightgown or something," said Steve. "I'll wait out here until you find out what the deal is."

"I don't think that's necessary," I said. "I'm sure she'll put me up for one night. If I need to make other long-term arrangements, I can do that tomorrow."

I got out of the car, and Steve came around to get my bag for me.

"You must have this thing loaded with bricks," he said with a tentative smile, in a weak attempt to bridge the distance between us.

"I'm used to the weight," I told him. "I've lugged it around all day. Thanks for meeting my plane. It was beyond the call of duty."

"I was glad to do it," said Steve. "It's great that you're back." He leaned down quickly and brushed my cheek with his lips. "If you need anything, just call. You know I still care about you, even if it's not quite the same as it used to be. Things change, and life goes on, and we roll with the punches. I had no way of knowing I was ever going to see you again."

I didn't respond to the statement or to the kiss, because I knew if I did I would start to cry. Instead I picked up my suitcase and started up the driveway. When I reached the sidewalk that ran in front of the condos, I turned and glanced back to see if his car was gone yet. It was still at the gate, and Steve was standing beside it. When he saw me looking back, he raised his hand and waved. Blinking back tears, I turned and kept on walking.

Lorelei's condominium was the last in the row, and I had to set my suitcase down twice before I got to it. When I reached it and pressed the buzzer, I was startled to hear a dog begin barking inside. After a moment Lorelei's voice called, "Get back from the door!"

I took a few steps backward to give her a chance to peer out through the peephole, which was something I didn't recall her ever doing before. Then I heard the click of the lock, and the door swung inward, revealing a woman I almost didn't recognize.

"So you came after all," she said. "That's what I expected. You're such a stubborn child, there's just no way to reason with you."

"Lorelei!" I whispered in horror. "Lorelei, what *happened*?"

"Don't stand there gaping," my grandmother said. "Come in."

The moment I was inside, she shut the door and locked it, while Porky raced around in circles, barking joyfully, hysterical with excitement about seeing me again.

I continued to stare incredulously at my grandmother. Her right arm was in an L-shaped cast that ran from her wrist to her armpit and the whole left side of her face was the yellowish color of a serious bruise in its final stages.

"What happened?" I asked again. "Were you in an accident?"

"It was no accident," said Lorelei. "I did something foolish. I opened my door to a stranger, and this is what happened." She sank down onto the sofa as though her legs were too tired to hold her, and I hurriedly sat down beside her and reached for her hand, bracing myself for what she was going to tell me.

"A week ago Pat called up from the gate to tell me a delivery man was here with a package," said Lorelei. "I told him to go ahead and send the man up with it. The Marshals Service has had several crates sent over here, so I thought this was just another one of those boxes.

"The man who arrived was very polite and gentlemanly. He asked me where I wanted him to put the box, and I told him to bring it inside and set it in the closet in the hall, which is where I've been storing your family's personal possessions. Once inside, though, he didn't head for the closet. His whole personality changed, and he suddenly got nasty. He told me he wanted to know where my son-in-law was hiding and if I didn't tell him I was going to be sorry."

"Then he wasn't connected with the Marshals Service at all?"

"Certainly not, but it took me a moment to realize it. As soon as I did, I made a dash for the bedroom. There's a phone extension in there, and I thought if I could get the door locked I could phone down to Pat and tell him I needed help. It was a good idea, and I actually think it might have worked, but I had just come back from a luncheon and was wearing heels. One of them caught on the edge of the carpet, and before I could regain my balance, the man had covered the distance between us and was on top of me. He threw me down, and my head crashed into the door frame. Then he grabbed my wrist and bent my arm up behind me."

"Oh, Lorelei, how dreadful!" I breathed. "Did you scream for help?"

"Of course I screamed, but it didn't do any good. One reason I bought a condo here at Golden Ridge was because they're so well insulated against noise. If I can't hear my neighbors, it stands to reason they can't hear me, so shrieking for help was an exercise in futility. If the windows had been open, it might have been different, but I had them closed because the air conditioner was on.

"The man kept twisting my arm, demanding to know where your father was, and it's lucky I didn't know or I might have told him. Finally I felt the bone snap. It's odd how you don't think of bones making noise when they break, but mine made a sound like a twig from a dried-out Christmas tree. The pain was so bad that I think I must have fainted, because the next thing I knew it was dark and I was lying in the hallway outside the bedroom. I managed somehow to get up and turn on the lights. I was very relieved to discover that I was alone."

"Oh, Lorelei!" I said again. I wanted to hug her, but I was afraid of the pain the pressure of my arms would cause her. "What did you do after that, call the police?"

"The police, the FBI, and an ambulance, in that order. At the hospital they set my arm and gave me a sedative. They kept me there overnight to make sure I didn't have a concussion, and the next day I was released and a friend drove me home. On the way, I had her stop at the kennel for Porky. I'm under no illusion this yapping beast is real protection, but at least he can bark and warn me if someone tries to break in."

"I can't believe we weren't even told," I said. "You'd think that Max could have gotten a message to us."

"He never even returned my call," said Lorelei. "His secretary told me the FBI takes no responsibility for people in the Witness Security Program and I should talk to the people at the U.S. Marshals Service. You do see, don't you, why it is that you can't move back here? The man who attacked me must finally have realized I didn't have the information he wanted, but there's no way he would ever believe that of you."

I had reached a point at which I could accept that statement. "You're right, I have to go back. I don't have a choice."

"Does anyone other than Steve know you're here?" asked Lorelei.

"His brother Billy, their parents maybe, and Sherry."

"Then we're going to have to leave tonight," said my grandmother.

"We?" I couldn't believe I had heard her correctly. "Did you say *we*?"

"I've been thinking about it ever since you phoned," said Lorelei. "I decided that if you came, I was going to go back with you. It wasn't an easy decision, because my roots are here—my friends, my activities, my memories of life with your grandfather. Still, such things are not as important as family. Your father's a sweet little boy who never grew up, and your mother lives in a world made of dreams and typing paper. It's my duty to be on call when the two of them need me."

"But you don't even know where we're living now," I said. "It's a little hick town in Florida called Grove City. They don't have a symphony there or a country club or anything. As far as I know, they don't even have a restaurant except for a McDonald's and the Cabbage Palm Grill."

"Then I won't bother taking my evening gowns," said Lorelei. "I can't pack a suitcase one-handed, so you're going to have to help me. We need to load the car and leave here immediately. The farther we get from Norwood tonight, the better."

There was one final question I felt compelled to ask her, despite the fact that I already knew the answer.

"Did the man who broke your arm have very dark eyes?"

"That's an understatement," said Lorelei. "They were pools of ink."

15

We were ready to leave in less than an hour. Lorelei directed while I did the packing. First I laid her matched luggage open on her bed; then I made a tour of the house with her, collecting items as she selected them, and carrying them back to the bedroom to load into the suitcases.

I was surprised at some of the things she chose to take with her. She stuck to her word about not taking her dinner dresses, but she did take an ermine stole and the contents of her jewelry box, a raw silk suit, and eight pairs of high-heeled shoes. The rest of her choices were sentimental—a doll with a porcelain face that dated back to her childhood, a family Bible, and a large assortment of photographs. One of the pictures was a small framed snapshot of Lorelei and my Grandpa Clyde on their honeymoon, smiling at each other on the balcony of a French hotel. They were dressed in old-fashioned clothing, but their faces were youthful and radiant, and they looked like stars in some old black and white movie. Another photo we packed was of my grandfather in his later years when his hair was sparse and his face was creased with smile lines. It brought back a jolting memory of Jim Peterson, and I determinedly shoved that vision out of my consciousness.

"That should do it," said Lorelei when the second suitcase had finally been closed and the buckles secured. "I can manage fine without the other things."

"But what about all your beautiful clothes!" I protested. "At least, let's try to pack the most expensive outfits."

"There's not enough room," Lorelei said matter-of-factly. "Remember, we're driving my car, not your mother's station wagon. We need to take the boxes I've stored for your parents, and as much as I shudder to think of it, we also have to allow enough space for Porky."

Lorelei's Porsche was parked in front of her condo. I loaded the trunk with the boxes from the hall closet and carried the suitcases out to put in the backseat. As I trudged back and forth with my cargo, Porky glued himself to my heels in quivering terror that he was going to be left behind again. On my third trip out to the car, he managed to slide in ahead of the luggage and wedge his stout body into the small slot of space between my overnight bag and one of Lorelei's suitcases. Heaving a sigh of relief, he made himself a nest there, so delighted to be coming with us that he didn't seem to care how uncomfortable he was.

After I had finished loading the car, I waited in the hallway while Lorelei made one last trip through the condo, checking windows and turning out lights. When she came back, she was carrying my tennis racket.

"Jodi brought this over after school let out," she said. "She told me this is the racket you like to use for tournaments."

"I can't play tournament tennis now," I said. "Dad's afraid I might get my picture in the paper."

"Really?" Lorelei said. "I hadn't thought about that, but I suppose it makes sense. It won't take up much space, so let's take it anyway. If nothing else, we can use it for keeping that dog in line."

To my amazement, my grandmother didn't look back. When we reached the car, I automatically started to get in on the passenger's side, but Lorelei surprised me by motioning me into the driver's seat.

"You do the driving," she said. "I'll act as navigator. I'm not accustomed to one-handed driving like you kids are, and the last thing we need right now is to be in an accident."

Three months earlier, in another lifetime, I would have been ecstatic at being allowed to drive Lorelei's Porsche. Ironically, now I didn't feel happy at all. I had returned home expecting my grandmother to put my life back in order in the bossy, capable manner I remembered from childhood. Having her hand me the keys to her cherished sports car indicated a role reversal I wasn't ready for.

When we pulled up to the gate, Pat stepped out of the guardhouse, glancing with obvious surprise at the overloaded car.

"You going on a trip, Mrs. Gilbert?" he asked Lorelei.

"A little vacation on my doctor's orders," she told him. "New England is so beautiful in the summertime, and my granddaughter flew in today so she could drive me up there."

"I'll keep a close watch on your place while you're gone," Pat said. "I want you to know, we've really upped the security. I'll never forgive myself for letting that man get in here. I should have suspected something and checked his credentials."

"I'm sure you would have found them in order," said Lorelei. "You had no way of knowing he wasn't who he said he was."

Pat pressed the switch to lift the gate, and as we pulled away I could see him in the rearview mirror, gazing after us with a puzzled expression on his face.

"He thinks we're crazy for leaving at night," I said.

"He probably does, but that can't be helped," said Lorelei. "I hope, if he's asked, he'll say we were headed for New England." She glanced at her watch. "We're doing well with our time, it's only eight thirty. We should be able to make it as far as the border tonight. There's a road map in the glove compartment, and I'll chart a route for us. We'll have to make this trip without using my credit cards, so before we leave we'd better stop at a bank."

It was while I was sitting in the car, waiting for Lorelei to withdraw money from the automatic teller, that I was hit with a feeling that somebody was watching us. There was no particular reason for my rush of nervousness. Still, I felt an indefinable pressure between my shoulder blades as though a beam of cold, harsh light were being focused there. I turned in my seat to look back through the car's rear window, and of course I didn't see a hollow-eyed vampire. Except for our car, positioned in front of the money machine, the well-lighted parking lot at Norwood Savings and Loan was empty.

I told myself I was simply being paranoid. There was no reason to think anybody would be tailing us. There hadn't been time for word to get out that I was back in town, and Lorelei had already been interrogated and discarded. Still, I was greatly relieved when my grandmother came back to the car and we were able to submerge ourselves in the Friday night traffic.

Lorelei's prediction that we would make it to North Carolina that night was wishful thinking. We had been on the road only three hours when the stress of the day caught up with me and I had to admit I couldn't keep going much longer. In Petersburg, Virginia, we stopped at a motel with a lighted Vacancy sign, and I waited in the car with Porky while Lorelei went in to register. Behind the office window a sleepy-looking desk clerk blinked in surprise when Lorelei paid him in cash. He handed her two keys, and she gave one back to him and asked a question that required a one-word answer. Then she came out to tell me that we would be staying in room 129 and the motel coffee shop opened at seven in the morning.

I drove the Porsche around to the rear of the motel, where I unloaded my overnight bag and the smaller of Lorelei's two suitcases. Released from his cramped quarters in the backseat, Porky headed straight for some bushes at the corner of the building. Then he came bounding back and broke into a frenzy of high-pitched barking at a black Camaro that had pulled into a parking space several units down from ours.

"We can't have this," said Lorelei. "Pets aren't allowed here. You're going to have to shut that dog in the car."

"He'll be all right once we get him inside," I promised.

"No, he won't," said Lorelei. "I know how he behaves. Every time somebody walks past the door, he'll start barking. Put him back in the car, and move it away from here. If it's parked at the back of the lot, he won't disturb people."

I moved the car as she asked, with an apology to Porky, who looked so dejected I could hardly bear to leave him. Then I went back to the room to rejoin Lorelei. Once we were secured for the night, exhaustion overwhelmed us, and we didn't even bother to turn on the television. Lorelei declined first use of the bathroom on the grounds that bathing with a cast on was such an ordeal that she didn't want to have to face it until morning. I was too grubby to go to bed without a shower, and the water felt so good I stayed under it for ages. When I finally returned to the bedroom, I found my grandmother, still fully dressed, stretched out asleep on one of the beds.

I stood for a moment, gazing down at her, shocked at how much she had aged since the last time I'd seen her. The bulk of the cast accentuated her fragility, and her fine-boned face, slack with sleep and without the benefit of makeup, showed lines and shadows that were usually concealed by cosmetics. Most startling of all, to me at least, was the fact that her honey blond hair was coming in at the roots a stony gray.

Carefully, so as not to wake her, I removed her shoes and placed them on the floor by her unopened suitcase. The room was turning cool from the air-conditioning. I tried to pull up the covers, but she was on top of them, so I took the spread off the second bed and laid it over her, experiencing once again the uncomfortable feeling that she had become the child, and I, the adult.

When I clicked off the overhead light and got into my own bed, I expected to sleep like a dead thing straight through until morning. Expected to, but didn't, for the moment the room went dark, I came abruptly awake, shot through with the same odd chill that I had experienced in the parking lot at the bank. It was late enough so there were no sounds from adjoining rooms to disturb me, but I had the feeling that someone was awake and aware, reaching out with his mind to touch me in the darkness.

Sliding out from under the sheet, I got out of bed and groped my way across the room to the door. When I placed my hand in its center, I knew instinctively that somebody on the far side was doing so also. Inches away, separated from me by nothing more than a wooden panel, someone was standing on the doorsill, trying to make a decision about what to do next. The drapes across the window were double thick, so he could not know for certain that our lights were off. Still, enough time had passed since we had entered the room for it to be reasonable to assume we were asleep.

I was suddenly acutely aware of how noisy our room was. Lorelei had started to snore, a sharp, rasping sound that overpowered the monotonous hum of the air conditioner, and the thud of my heartbeat crashed like a drum in my ears, so loud that I was sure it could be heard for miles. Then I heard the most frightening sound of all, the scrape of something metalic being cautiously slipped into the keyhole. My mind flew back to the sight of Lorelei in the office, refusing the second key that was being offered her. The desk clerk had obviously realized there were two in our party. If someone had gone to him later and identified himself as Lorelei's companion, the clerk would not have thought twice about giving him the duplicate.

All this flashed through my mind in the fraction of a second it took for my hand to fly up and hit the deadbolt. The bolt slid into place with a sound like a gunshot, and without pausing for an instant, I leapt to the window and jerked aside the draperies. The security light by our door illuminated the section of pavement in front of the motel unit, but beyond that on either side lay pools of darkness. From what I could see, the sidewalk appeared to be empty.

In the room behind me, Lorelei continued to snore, undisturbed by my sudden burst of activity. Had anything actually happened, or had I imagined it? Was there a figure out there crouched in the darkness, or was I inventing terrors that had no substance? When I strained my eyes and stared hard into one of the shadow pockets, I could almost believe I could see a shift in the blackness as though there were somebody there who was changing position.

I let the curtain fall back into place, and in the deluge of heavier darkness the lighted dial on the telephone on the table between the beds glowed softly. I crossed the room to the phone and dialed the office. After a dozen rings, I hung up the receiver. I could only suppose the Vacancy sign was now off and the weary clerk had finally retired for the night.

By this time I was too charged with adrenaline to sleep. I got back into bed and lay there, rigidly alert, with my ears attuned for the slightest rustle at the door. Hours passed, while dawn crept closer and closer, and my mind churned with visions of vampire faces at the window and blood-stained talons picking surreptitiously at door locks. It wasn't until I heard people beginning to stir in the units on either side of our own that I was finally able to relax enough to doze off for a while.

I awoke several hours later to the sound of water running in the bathroom and opened my eyes to find that the bed across from me was empty. Dragging myself out of bed, I pulled on my clothes and opened the door of our room to a blue and gold morning and the realization that it was much later than it ought to be. Except for the black Camaro that Porky had reacted to so violently, the cars on our side of the lot had all departed, and two girls in shorts were pushing a housekeeping cart along the sidewalk and dashing into rooms with clean towels and sheets.

I shut the door behind me and walked around the side of the building to the office. When I entered, I found that the clerk from the night before had been replaced by a plump young woman with frizzy hair.

"Good morning!" she chirped in greeting. "What can I do for you?"

"My grandmother and I are in room one twenty-nine," I told her. "We're getting ready to leave and can find only one room key. Neither of us can remember how many we had. Is there a second key we ought to be looking for?"

"I don't know," said the girl. "I just came on duty this morning. I'll check and see if any of the duplicates are missing." She turned to inspect a board of pegs on the wall. "No, as far as I can tell, they're all here."

"Good," I said. "Then we don't have to do a room search." The relief in my voice was far from manufactured.

After leaving the office I stopped by the car to get Porky, who immediately made a dash for his favorite bushes. Then I took him back to the room, where Lorelei, now bathed and dressed, was putting on lipstick.

"I thought that's where you'd gone," she said, nodding at Porky. "I hope he didn't chew up everything in the car."

"Of course not," I said. "That's not one of Porky's vices."

"It's nice to know he has one redeeming feature," said Lorelei.

She finished putting on makeup without assistance, but allowed me to help with the buttons on her dress. Then I carried our bags back to the Porsche, and after checking out at the office, we drove around to have breakfast in the coffee shop. We were lucky enough to be seated next to a window, and the bright morning sunlight poured in across our table, flooding our plates and cups with molten gold. The coffee was hot and strong, and the rolls rich with cinnamon, and suddenly everything seemed much better than it had been. I considered telling Lorelei about my panic attack in the night, but the light of day made the whole adventure seem laughable. What was there to be gained by frightening my grandmother with a story about something I'd probably only imagined? It wasn't as though a key to our room had been missing. Everything at the office had been in order. There was always the possibility that the duplicate key had been borrowed and then returned, but it was far more likely it hadn't been taken at all.

So I sat and enjoyed breakfast with my grandmother, who was making a heroic effort to put the past behind her. When we got back in the car we made the discovery that we must have inadvertently packed the road map in one of our suitcases, so we had to stop at a service station to get another one. Our departure was further delayed by a stop at a convenience store to buy dog food, so it was after nine before we were finally under way. We stopped at noon for lunch at a Howard Johnson's and twenty minutes later were back on the road again.

It wasn't until midafternoon that I happened to glance in the rearview mirror to see that the car behind us was a black Camaro.

16

There are thousands of Camaros in the world, and out of that many, a significant number must be black. It was nothing more than coincidence that the car that happened to be behind us on the freeway was the same make and color as one of the many cars that had been parked at our motel.

I recited those statements over and over in my mind as I worked to get the rearview mirror repositioned so it would reflect the person at the wheel. The problem was that the car was too far back. I glanced across at Lorelei in the seat beside me. Lulled by the rhythm of the road and the monotony of the scenery, she had nodded off soon after lunch and was now napping peacefully with her head tilted back against the headrest. I hated to disturb her for something as insignificant as another black car in a world that was filled with such vehicles. First, I thought, I would try to draw the Camaro closer and see if I could get a look at the driver.

Experimentally, I eased up on the accelerator, letting my speed drop slowly from sixty-five to forty in hopes that the Camaro would decide to pull out and pass me. Instead, it too slowed down, continuing to hang well back, but still keeping pace with the travel speed of the Porsche. I accelerated, and the Camaro sped up also, although there was nothing strange about that, I reminded myself. It was natural when driving the freeway to pace yourself according to the car ahead of you. Actually, I had been doing the same thing myself. The Chevy station wagon in front of us had been doing a steady sixty-five for the past fifty miles, and I had been adjusting my cruising speed to coincide with that. If the Chevy had suddenly increased its speed to seventy, I would automatically have done so also in order to keep the distance between us constant.

Deciding to see what would happen if I altered the pattern, I abruptly changed lanes and pressed the accelerator down almost to the floorboard. The engine roared as the transmission snapped into high and the Porsche went shooting past the lumbering station wagon. The occupants, a man and woman and three children, all turned to gape at us with shocked disapproval as we left them lingering behind in a cloud of exhaust fumes.

I continued bearing down on the accelerator and watched the needle on the speedometer creep higher and higher until it seemed that the Porsche was on its way to becoming airborne.

The burst of speed had jolted Lorelei awake, and she leaned against her shoulder harness to regard me with bewilderment. "What in the world do you think you're doing, April!"

"I'm sorry," I told her. "I didn't mean to wake you. I wanted to see if that car back there was tailing us."

I glanced in the mirror to see if the Camaro had passed the station wagon and was following me at the speed at which I was now driving. It wasn't, but someone else was, which didn't surprise me, for I heard the siren one instant before I saw the patrol car.

"Of all the luck!" I muttered. "This *would* happen *now*!"

"What did you expect?" snapped Lorelei. "You're driving like a maniac!"

With a sigh of resignation, I reduced my speed to a point where it was possible to pull over onto the shoulder of the road. The patrol car came to a stop several yards behind us, and the officer got out and came over to confront me.

"I'd like to see your driver's license," he told me. As I took it out of my wallet, he continued, "To say you were over the speed limit is putting it mildly. I clocked you at nearly ninety. May I see your registration, too, please? This is a lot of car for a kid your age to be driving."

"This happens to be my car, young man," Lorelei informed him with dignity. "My granddaughter is driving it for me because I've had an injury."

"I'm sorry, ma'am," the officer responded politely. "I'm afraid, though, it's our policy to check registration. Cars like this one have a habit of disappearing from their owners' driveways. If that happened to yours, I'm sure you'd be happy we do this."

So Lorelei hauled the registration out of the glove compartment, and I handed over Valerie Weber's driver's license. Then we waited while the patrolman checked both documents and took them back to his car to radio headquarters. In the meantime, the Chevy station wagon passed us, creeping along at a snail's pace in honor of the patrol car, and I caught a snapshot glimpse of the family inside it, glaring self-righteously out at us through the side windows.

The officer returned with our documents and wrote out a speeding ticket.

"I see you've had your license only a month," he said. "It's a rite of passage for every new driver to have a fender bender, but if you continue to drive like this you'll end up in the morgue."

I murmured a few contrite statements and accepted the ticket.

A few minutes later, when we were back on the freeway,

Lorelei suddenly said, "You may have been right about that car. It should have passed us while we were stopped, but it didn't."

"There was an exit a mile or so back," I said. "He might have gotten off there."

"Or he might have pulled over and waited so he wouldn't lose us by getting ahead of us. If that's the case, he'll probably try to catch up with us."

We fell into silence, both watching the road behind us. Sure enough, it was not long before the black Camaro came into view, barreling along well over the speed limit in the fast left lane. It started slowing down before it came abreast of us and then casually shifted over into our lane, pacing itself behind us as though it had been there always, attached to our rear bumper by an invisible cable.

"There should be another exit coming up soon," said Lorelei. "He won't be expecting you to take it. That's probably our best chance of getting away from him. Pull over into the fast lane and start speeding up. You may be able to trick him into overshooting it."

I nodded, following her meaning without need for elaboration. This time when I changed lanes, the Camaro did too. I again began to accelerate, keeping an eye on the car in the mirror, as the Camaro increased its speed to keep it consistent with ours. It was close enough now so I could see that the driver was a man who was wearing sunglasses. The exit to Weston Road loomed up ahead of us, but I didn't brake to indicate that I was aware of it. Instead, I checked in the mirror to make sure that all the lanes to my right were empty and continued to increase speed until we were practically flying. Then, without hitting the turn signal, I whispered a prayer and gave the steering wheel a hard twist to the right. The Porsche leapt diagonally across the three vacant lanes and landed on the exit ramp, where it went careening around the loop like a walnut in a Mixmaster.

I was so occupied with the task of keeping the car on the road that I didn't dare lift my eyes to look in the mirror.

"What happened?" I managed to gasp. "Is he still behind us?"

Lorelei swiveled her head. "I think he missed the exit." I could tell she was having to struggle to keep her voice steady.

I let the car lose momentum before touching the brake and then gradually began to tap it down into a manageable speed. It wasn't until we were stopped at a four-way light that I discovered I had been gripping the steering wheel so tightly the blood had left my fingers. I peeled my hands off the wheel and flexed them to get the circulation going again, and then, feeling a little light-headed but back in control, I turned left onto Weston Road and drove at a sensible and legal thirty miles an hour into Tutterville, South Carolina.

Tutterville, with its tree-lined streets and neat pastel houses, resembled a movie set for a G-rated film laid in Normaltown, U.S.A. Everywhere you looked there were men washing cars in their driveways and housewives in shorts and halter tops pruning roses. Children romped in sprinklers, and older people, who could have served as a cast for the movie *Cocoon*, were rocking on porches or chatting with neighbors on sun-dappled sidewalks. It was a restful, summer Saturday in a town so postcard-perfect that danger seemed a concept too ridiculous to contemplate.

"Maybe we just imagined it," I said shakily. "Maybe he wasn't following us at all."

"He was following us," said Lorelei. "No two ways about it. He must have been right on our tail when we left the condo."

"But how could he have known we were leaving?" I asked. "I hadn't been in Norwood more than two hours."

"Obviously, my phone was tapped," said Lorelei. "He heard you say you were coming and was ready for whatever we decided to do next."

Her down-to-earth acceptance of what had happened convinced me she was tougher than I'd thought, and I decided to share the experience I had been withholding.

"Last night I thought I heard someone trying to get into our room," I said. "When I looked out the window, nobody seemed to be out there. I checked at the office this morning, and no keys were missing. I've been trying to make myself believe I only imagined it."

"Maybe you did, and maybe you didn't," said Lorelei. "Doors can be opened with other devices than keys. The important thing now is we seem to have shaken the Camaro. The driver must have a low opinion of our intelligence or he wouldn't have taken the risk of following so closely. I imagine now he'll expect us to keep driving south and to get back onto the freeway the next chance we get." She was silent a moment as she studied the road map. "What I think we should do is reverse directions and take the state highway north instead of south."

Relieved to have the decision made for me, I did as she suggested and drove north on Highway 15 to a town called St. George. There we reentered the freeway and drove back south again for four more hours until we crossed the state border into Florida and stopped at a motel in St. Augustine for the night.

At least, that was our plan. It didn't work out that way. After we checked into our room and I napped for an hour, Lorelei and I had dinner at a seafood restaurant. Then we returned to our room, and I brought in our bags.

That was when we realized something was missing. It was Lorelei who first became aware of it as she rummaged through her suitcase.

"I don't have the map," she said. "Is it in your bag?"

"No," I said. "I thought it got packed in yours."

There was a pause. Then my grandmother said, "Make a search for it. Maybe it got shoved down under some of your clothes."

"I know I don't have it," I said. "We must have left it in Petersburg. Does it really matter? There's a second map in the car."

"That's not the point," said Lorelei. "I marked our route on the original map. If it didn't get packed, then it must have been left in our room."

"You mean—you think—" I realized where she was headed and felt a sharp taloned hand close over my heart. "You think that man may have gotten into our motel room?"

"The maids were doing the housekeeping chores when we left, and the doors to all the units were standing open. Anybody could have walked into any one of them. We must have been in the coffee shop half an hour. That was plenty of time for someone to have checked our room to see if we'd left anything meaningful behind."

"But if he'd had a marked map, he wouldn't have had to follow us," I said. "Wouldn't he just have driven on through to Grove City?"

"He'd still have had to locate your parents when he got there," said Lorelei. "He doesn't know where they live or what name they're using. It would take time to find that out, and since he knew we were headed there anyway, the simplest thing would have been to let us lead him."

"Newcomers stand out in a town that small," I said. "If he asks around, he's bound to find someone who's noticed us."

On the screen of my mind I saw my parents and Jason, seated in the living room playing Monopoly, with the figure of a vampire poised in the doorway. Or worse, the creature would come for them while they were sleeping. I pictured the front door swinging silently inward while the fans in the windows covered the sound of footsteps. As always, the doors to the bedrooms would be standing open to the hall to allow the air to circulate through the house. Mike Vamp could walk straight into my parents' bedroom without even having to place his hand on the doorknob.

By the time I had gotten that far, the phone receiver was in my hand and I was frantically dialing the number of our house in Grove City. The phone rang over and over without an answer.

"They're out," I said. "That's odd, because they never go anywhere."

"Maybe they've gone to a friend's house," Lorelei suggested.

"They don't have friends," I said. "They keep to themselves."

We sat on the motel beds, across from each other, each seeing her panic reflected in the eyes of the other.

"Nothing has happened to anybody yet," said Lorelei, trying to make the statement sound reassuring. "Even if he drove nonstop from the time we left the freeway at Tutterville, there hasn't been time for him to have reached Grove City."

"Tom Geist is the person to call, but his number's unlisted," I said. "We have it at home, taped to the base of the telephone, but I never thought of copying it and carrying it with me. I guess we'd better get back in the car and start driving."

"You're worn out," said Lorelei. "We've been on the road all day. I'll drive the first few hours so you can rest."

"You can't do that with that cast on your arm," I objected. "You said yourself you can't manage one-handed driving."

"I retract that statement," said Lorelei. "I'll manage fine. It can't be as dangerous as your daredevil stunt on the freeway. Besides, we don't have a choice. If we don't warn your parents, that monster who broke my arm may injure your mother."

So we got back into the car and took off again, with Lorelei driving the first two hours, and me, the second two.

As the road unrolled like a long, black ribbon before us, I comforted myself with the knowledge that when the Camaro arrived in Grove City the driver would still not know how to find our house. Even if he were able to get our address, the lack of street signs and curbside numbers would make it almost impossible to locate it at night. We'd had a hard enough time finding it ourselves, even with written directions and a map to guide us.

About five miles short of Grove City we hit the rain. At first it was only a spatter of drops on the windshield, but it grew increasingly heavier until by the time we reached the town limits the heavens had opened, and I couldn't see more than a couple of yards in front of me. It was late enough so there were no other cars on the road as I inched the Porsche down the river that had once been Orange Avenue, guided by the blur of water-curtained streetlights. I missed the entrance to Lemon Lane completely and had to make a U-turn to go back and search for it. When I finally did find the road and turn the car onto it, Lorelei stared out her window into the immensity of the darkness like a traveler in space who's been sucked into a black hole.

"There really are houses along here?" she asked doubtfully.

"A few," I told her. "They're back behind the trees."

"This rain is probably a blessing in disguise," she said. "It's hard to imagine anyone locating anything in this downpour unless he knew exactly where he was going."

Even I had trouble finding our house, and it was with relief that I finally spotted the mailbox. When I eased the Porsche into the narrow mouth of the driveway, I became aware of a strange, dark shape at the side of it. It took me a moment to recognize what it was, and when I did a scream rose into my throat and hung there, caught, unable to move any farther. Yanking the steering wheel hard, I sent our car spinning around in a half-moon curve so it shot off the drive and plowed through a thicket of palmetto shrubs to come to a stop facing back toward the road.

There, in the beam of our headlights, was my parents' Plymouth, nose down in the surging waters that swept through the drainage ditch.

17

Before the engine had stopped running, I was out of the Porsche and down on my knees at the edge of the embankment, straining to see into the water-filled interior of the car. What had happened was all too obvious; whoever had been driving the Plymouth had neglected to center it at the point where the driveway narrowed to bridge the ditch, and the left front wheel had slipped off the edge of the driveway, so the car had taken the plunge diagonally and was now positioned hood down with the rear end elevated.

"Whose car is that?" asked Lorelei, materializing beside me. I could tell by her voice that she'd already guessed the answer.

"It's ours," I said, "but there isn't anybody in it."

"Thank God for that!" exclaimed Lorelei. "But someone *was* in it! One or both of your parents and maybe Bram."

"It was Mother," I said. "I'm sure the driver was Mother." The knowledge rose up to confront me, stark and unavoidable. "Mother's started drinking since we've been in Florida, not just on special occasions, but all the time. She's been so unhappy, so frustrated about her writing. We've none of us wanted to recognize it, so we've closed our eyes to it."

Scrambling up from the ground, I broke into a run back across the yard to the house. The waterlogged steps of the porch gave beneath my feet like rotten sponges as I pounded up them with Porky at my heels. When I groped for the doorknob, I found the front door was already open, as though the last one through it had been in too much of a hurry to close it behind him.

The house was dark, and my hand shot up to the wall switch. With a click, the living room leapt into existence, the cream-color walls that Mother had recently painted a striking contrast to the shabby furnishings and the sun-bleached curtains at the windows. The room was just as it had been when I had left except that the Sunday paper had been tossed on the sofa and the coffee table held a Coke can and what appeared to be a half-empty glass of orange juice.

Porky paused to shake himself, but I dashed on down the hall, snapping on lights as I ran, driving the pervasive darkness out of each room in turn. None of the rooms was occupied, and the neatly made bed in my parents' room had obviously not been slept in. Jason's bed was a mess, but that didn't mean anything, since he almost never made his bed in the morning, and Mother only did it for him on the one day a week she took the sheets to the launderette. In the kitchen, Mother's typewriter was set up on the table with manuscript pages scattered around it like dry leaves in autumn. My eyes flew automatically to the door of the refrigerator, which was where we always left notes for each other, but it didn't hold any message. On the counter beside the telephone, however, there lay a scrap of paper that told as much of the story as I needed to know. Jotted on it in my mother's familiar handwriting was Kim Stanfield's telephone number.

Immediately, I realized what must have happened. Somehow Mother had learned I was not at Kim's house. Since Kim was not in town to tell her, the only person who could have given me away was Larry. Jason had said he'd attempted to reach me on Thursday, and his ego must have been dented when I didn't return his call. Perhaps he had followed up with a call on Sunday and Mother had told him I'd gone to Kim's for the weekend. Larry's response would have been to say that was impossible since Kim had gone to Miami with her family.

The scenario rolled through my mind, so clear and immediate it was hard to believe I had not been there to see it—Mother phoning Kim's house and, getting no answer, rushing out to the car to drive herself over there. Had she gone alone, or had Dad and Jason been with her? And had anyone been hurt when the car went into the ditch? Was there anybody in town who would know what had happened?

Stricken with guilt and panic, I grabbed for the telephone and dialed the only local number I could think of. The phone seemed to ring interminably before it was answered and a man's unfamiliar voice mumbled a groggy "Hello?"

"Please, may I speak to Larry?" I asked in a rush.

"To Larry?" the man said irritably. "Who is this anyway? Don't you know it's one o'clock in the morning?"

"I'm Val Weber, a friend of Larry's," I told him. "I'm sorry to call at this hour, but it's terribly important."

"Weber?" the man said. "I've heard that name. You must be one of the people that guy who called here earlier was trying to get hold of."

"Somebody tried to call us at your house?" I asked weakly.

"The guy who phoned Larry said he was looking for some people by the name of Corrigan. He called at midnight and woke up the whole blasted family. I heard Larry ask him if those 'Corrigans' might be going by the name of

'Weber' and have a daughter who plays tennis and a son with two-color eyes. I don't know what kind of game you people are playing, but I've got to be at work at seven in the morning, and I don't appreciate being waked up twice in one night."

"Please, Mr. Bushnell, let me speak to Larry," I begged. "I've got to know what else he may have told that man. Did he give him directions about how to find our house?"

"You can ask him that in the morning," the man said firmly. "I'm not going to wake my kid up again tonight."

The phone clunked hard in my ear and was replaced by the dial tone. Behind me Porky's toenails clicked rhythmically against the weathered kitchen linoleum as he came trotting in to explore the room.

From the living room Lorelei's voice called, "April? Where are you?"

"In the kitchen, using the phone," I called back to her, trying to make a decision as to what to do next. My first thought was to call the police for protection, but how could I convince them of the extent of our danger? Since I wasn't allowed to tell them we were in the Security Program, they would think my fears were excessive and ridiculous. The only person who would understand was Tom, and for all I knew, my father might already have phoned him. When Dad found out I'd run off, he was sure to have guessed I was headed for Norwood, and the reasonable thing to have done was inform Tom Geist.

I had just picked up the phone and was in the process of turning it upside down so I could read the number taped to its base when Porky suddenly burst into a volley of barking. It was the high-pitched, staccato sort of yapping that usually meant he had spotted something strange and exciting. When I glanced at him I saw that his head was lifted and his eyes were riveted to the far side of the room at about the level of my shoulder. I turned to follow his gaze and gasped in horror. There, behind the rain-streaked pane of the kitchen window, was the face of a vampire.

I could not move. I was not capable of screaming. All I could do was stand there, frozen with shock, as the reincarnation of my worst childhood nightmare stared back at me. His lips were pressed tightly together, but the corners of his mouth were curved upward in a smile that was almost as horrible as if he had been displaying fangs. He might have come straight out of *The Lost Boys* or *Salem's Lot,* but I knew that he was more dangerous than any fictional character.

This was the real-life bloodchaser—this was the hitman.

Lorelei spoke from behind me. "Porky, be quiet! You'll raise the dead with that infernal barking. Whom are you calling, April, the police or the hospital?"

Her voice broke the spell, and I was able to move again. The phone fell out of my hands and crashed to the floor as I dashed across the kitchen to the outside door. I shoved the lock into place and whirled to face my grandmother.

"The front door!" I cried. "Did you lock it when you came in?"

"Probably not," said Lorelei. "I was in such a hurry to see if your mother was here that I didn't even think about it. What's the matter? Why is Porky barking?"

"He's there at the window!" I told her. "Don't you see him?" I gestured toward the glass, but the face was gone. All that could now be seen was a world of blackness, alive with the eerie movement of wind-tossed tree branches.

"I'll go lock it now," said Lorelei. "You phone the police. Tell them a prowler is trying to break into the house."

She started back down the hall, but I tore past her, knowing I'd let too much time go by already. The front door was not only unlocked, it was standing open, and as I had feared, the living room was no longer empty. The man with the vampire face stood framed in the doorway, backlit by a brilliant sledge blow of lightning. He was tall and lean, and his water-soaked T-shirt accentuated the long, hard muscles in his arms and shoulders that made the gun in his hands an unnecessary accessory. This time there was no blond wig to cover his thick, dark hair, but I recognized the piercing black eyes immediately.

"What do you think you're doing here?" I demanded.

"I'm here to visit your father," Mike Vamp told me. His voice was low-pitched and cultured, almost a purr, which seemed to reassure Porky, who stopped his barking and started instead to wag his tail in greeting. "I presume you're April—or perhaps you'd prefer to be called Valerie? People seem to have trouble knowing how to refer to you."

"That's the man!" Lorelei said from the doorway. "He's the one who attacked me!"

"How are you tonight, Mrs. Gilbert?" the hitman asked her. "What a pleasant surprise that we meet again so soon. I trust your arm is mending the way it should be?"

Lorelei did a magnificent job of concealing her emotions. "If you have any sense, you'll get out of here," she said. "My granddaughter's called the police, and they'll be here any minute now."

"Oh, I rather doubt that," said Mike Vamp. "There wasn't enough time. I saw her drop the phone before she started dialing." He came farther into the room and closed the door, shutting out the incessant beat of the rain.

"If it's Dad you want, he's not here," I told him defiantly. "We can't tell you where he is, because we just got here."

"I'm aware of that," he said. "My car is parked at the side of the house, and I sat and watched as you pulled in the driveway. I thought at first it might be your parents returning, but then, from the lights, I realized it had to be the Porsche. I must admit I was surprised to see you. I hadn't expected you ladies to drive straight through."

"How were you able to find the house?" asked Lorelei. "We hardly found it ourselves in the rain and darkness."

"I had directions," Vamp told her. "During your phone conversation with your granddaughter, she mentioned a friend named Larry Bushnell. There was only one listing for Bushnell in the phone book. Larry didn't seem very happy with you, April. When I told him I was a federal agent tracking down an embezzler, he was more than willing to do his patriotic duty. I didn't have any problem finding the house."

"How did you find us in Richmond?" The question burst out of its own accord, and I braced myself for the answer I didn't want to hear.

"It was your letter, of course, in your boyfriend's mailbox. That was the first piece of mail he'd received in a week, so I figured there was a good chance that it was from you. The postmark gave me the city, and you said you were on the fourteenth floor, which narrowed down the number of hotels I had to check before I found a family that got all their meals through room service."

"What are you planning to do with us?" asked Lorelei. "There can't be any reason to harm my granddaughter."

"She's served her purpose," said Vamp. "She brought me here. Her only use to me now is as a hostage. Family men like Corrigan turn into pussycats when they hear their beloved children pleading and crying."

"I told you, Dad's gone," I said. "We don't know where."

"That's quite all right," said Vamp. "I don't mind waiting."

"For all we know, he may not be coming back here!"

"I think he will." He gave me his tight-lipped smile. "This is his nest, and he's bound to return eventually."

"This is all so crazy!" I cried. "Dad doesn't know anything! He never had evidence against anybody but Loftin!"

"The people I work for don't take chances," said the hitman. "Too many lives are involved and too much is at stake. I'm going to have to stash you ladies somewhere.

April, you're familiar with the house. Why don't you take your grandma and me on a tour of it?"

So we walked down the hall together, with stupid Porky romping ahead of us, still wagging his tail. I'd passed the point of fear and had settled into numbness, as though I had no connection with what was happening. Visions of people I loved leapt into my mind as if each one had come to bid me good-bye. I saw Dad's gentle smile and hopeful expression as he suggested our ill-fated trip to Disney World. I saw Mother at the typewriter, lost in a world of her own creation, and Jason, his small face radiant after *Song of the South.* I saw Steve and Jodi and Sherry, and I even saw Jim Peterson with his craggy face and his arms piled high with packages.

Jim—I whispered silently—Jim, I'm so sorry! I'm the one who did it, I called in the vampire. I was stupid and selfish and caused a tragedy to happen, and now, God help me, I've done the same thing again.

It was dumb, Jim said, and I actually heard his voice as clear and kind as though he were walking beside me. *You're a kid from the Cinemax generation, April. You can't believe real-life stories don't all have happy endings. You were dumb, all right, but dumb's not the same as stupid. You've got a brain, so get on the ball and use it.*

Our tour was abruptly over at the end of the hallway.

"I don't care which room you lock us in," I said dully. "A bathroom, kitchen, bedroom, it doesn't matter. Whatever you do, though, please don't make it a closet. I can't stand being shut in a place without windows."

"I'm afraid you won't have much of a choice," said Vamp. I didn't need to look to know he was smiling. "I'm going to have to barricade the door, and only the closets have doors that open outward."

We ended up in the walk-in closet in my parents' room, jabbed by hangers and nearly smothered by clothing. As we heard the sound of the dresser being shoved against the door, Lorelei said bitterly, "He took such joy in doing this. You should never have told him you have claustrophobia. This is a man who gets pleasure from making people suffer."

"I know," I said. "But things aren't as bad as they might be. Brer Fox doesn't know it yet, but he's thrown us in the briar patch."

18

I reached up and groped for the string that triggered the closet light. It took me a while to find it, and I was beginning to panic at the thought that it might have broken or come loose from the overhead fixture when it suddenly brushed my hand like the edge of a cobweb, and I grabbed it and pulled.

The bulb went on, and my grandmother's face appeared inches from my own, taut with a combination of fear and exhaustion.

Still, she managed to ask calmly, "What's that about a briar patch?"

"It's from one of the old Disney movies," I told her. "Brer Rabbit wants to escape from his enemy, the fox. He knows that whatever he asks, Brer Fox will do the opposite, so he tells him—"

"You don't have to recite the story of Uncle Remus to me," said Lorelei. "I was reading it to your mother forty years ago. Why did you want that man to shut us in a closet?"

"Because the closets in this house have escape hatches," I said, pointing at the ceiling directly above us, where a rectangular piece of plywood was set into the plaster.

"I see," she murmured thoughtfully. "A trapdoor to the attic. But what possible good will it do us for you to climb up there? Won't that be exchanging one prison for another?"

"There's a door in the closet in Bram's room too," I told her. "He and his friends climb up and use the attic for a hideout. If I can get across and climb down into his room, I may be able to escape from the house and get help."

"Are you going to be able to get up there?" Lorelei asked doubtfully. "There's nothing in the closet you can use for a stepladder, and with my arm like it is, I can't even give you a boost."

"That won't be a problem," I said. "Getting up will be easy. The part I'm worried about is getting back down."

I made a hasty survey of the contents of the closet. As Lorelei said, it contained nothing but clothing, but the clothes bar was firmly attached to supports behind the walls and appeared to be sturdy enough to bear my weight. Taking a pair of Dad's trousers down from their hanger, I slung them across the bar so they straddled it with one of the legs hanging down on either side. Then I knotted the cuffs together to form a loop and inserted my foot as though I were mounting a horse. Catching hold of the edge of the shelf at the top of the closet, I straightened until I was standing upright in the stirrup with my shoulders braced against the trapdoor above me. When I shoved against the partition, it lifted easily, and within minutes I had hauled myself up into the attic.

Heat and dampness poured over me like a tidal wave, along with the pungent odors of bananas and peanut butter. The open trapdoor allowed enough light to filter up from the closet so I could see for several feet, but beyond that limited area there was absolute blackness.

Lorelei called up to me softly, "Is everything all right?"

"There's not as much room as I'd hoped there would be," I told her. "I thought it would be a full attic that you could stand up in, but at this end, at least, it's not much more than a crawl space. I can't understand why those boys like to play up here. It's like a real-life setting for Dungeons and Dragons."

I stared into the darkness, trying to get oriented. I knew the general direction of Jason's room, but without any landmarks to guide me, it was hard to gauge distance. To make matters worse, the floor wasn't boarded over, but was composed of narrow beams connected by sheets of plywood so flimsy I was afraid to put my weight on them. It was hard to imagine how my brother and his friends had managed to play there without crashing down through the ceiling to land on top of us.

I drew a deep breath and, praying I could keep from falling, began to inch my way along the network of planking on my hands and knees. My chief concern was to move as silently as possible. I tried to visualize the pattern of the rooms beneath me—my parents' bedroom, the hallway, the bathroom, and Jason's room. Where in the house would Vamp be now? I asked myself, and decided he was probably in the living room, since from there he would be able to watch from the window and see the lights of a car pulling into the driveway.

The roof peaked at the center of the attic, allowing me enough head space so I could stand up and walk. That proved harder than crawling, however, since I had to bend double at the waist, which made it almost impossible to keep my balance on the beams. Regretfully, I returned to my hands and knees and continued on in that manner until I felt the ceiling brush the top of my head at the exact same angle it had above my parents' closet. Since Jason's room was the mirror image of theirs, I could only assume his closet lay just ahead of me.

I crawled on for several more feet but couldn't find the door. I ran my hands across the plywood sheeting between the support planks, but found neither cracks nor any indication of a handle. What I did come in contact with was an open-face peanut butter sandwich that stuck to my hand as though it were spread with glue, and next to that, a bunch of overripe bananas and a cellophane sack that had evidently once contained cookies.

The fact that I'd come upon Jason's stash of food supplies gave me hope that I was not too far from the door. I continued to fumble around in all directions, but all I had to show for my efforts were splinters. Then my knuckles bumped against something metallic. I slid my hand across the cylindrical object, and my heart gave a leap as my thumb encountered a button. It was like being handed an unexpected present. My brother had left me the best gift of all, a flashlight.

I pressed the switch, and the world jumped into place. The trap door I was searching for was diagonally across from me, just far enough away so I hadn't been able to locate it. A nail had been driven partway into it to form a handle, and when I gripped it and pulled, the door swung easily upward. Although Jason's closet light wasn't on, the rectangular opening was illuminated by a faint yellow glow, and when I leaned over to peer down into it, I saw that both the closet and bedroom doors were open and the darkness was being diluted by light from the hall.

Perched on the beam that ran parallel to the opening, I let my legs dangle down into the space below me. Then, lowering myself until I was partially supported by the clothes bar, I allowed myself to drop the rest of the way to the floor.

Because I was wearing tennis shoes, I landed softly, like a cat dropping out of a tree onto a cushion of grass. When I emerged from the closet into my brother's room, my first choice would have been to escape through the window, but

Jason's window was as small as the one in my room, and even he could not have squeezed through it.

That left me no alternative but to leave by a door. If, as I supposed, Mike Vamp had positioned himself by the window at the front of the house, the only escape route left to me was through the kitchen. Turning off the flashlight, but still gripping it tightly, I crept across the room to the doorway and stood there listening for sounds from the living room. When I didn't hear any, I thrust a tentative foot out into the hall and paused again, made more nervous than ever by the oppressive silence. Cautiously I eased my way into the hall, hating the thought of being so exposed and vulnerable. A floorboard creaked, and I almost jumped through the ceiling, but to my relief there was still no response from the living room. It was as though I were being granted some special dispensation that permitted me to move through the house unnoticed.

Creeping down the hall, I slipped into the kitchen. The overhead light was still on, and on the floor at the base of the counter lay the telephone I had dropped when I'd seen the face at the window. The receiver was off the hook and beeping urgently like a small, dependent child torn away from its mother. The sound seemed to bounce off the walls and echo through the house. It was hard to imagine how anyone could ignore it.

When I crossed the room to the back door, I was momentarily disconcerted to find that it was no longer locked, but I didn't give myself time to absorb the significance of that fact. The exciting knowledge that freedom was that close was so intoxicating it dulled my ability to reason. Lulled into a sense of security by my luck so far, I yanked open the door and stepped out into the yard.

At some point since our arrival, the rain had stopped. Like most Florida storms, this one had ended abruptly, leaving in its wake a calm, wet world, filled with the song of frogs cavorting in puddles and the high-pitched sawing of crickets hidden in the underbrush. High in the sky a thin, bleached moon peeped shyly out through a hole in the clouds, slimmer than it had been the night of Amy's party and guarded on either side by an entourage of stars.

I was halfway down the steps when Porky started barking. My first reaction was to wonder what could have triggered him. If he hadn't heard me drop down into Jason's closet, it seemed strange that he would react to my slipping from the house. It took me a moment to realize he wasn't inside and the barking was coming, instead, from the yard to my left. An instant later, I saw a pale blur streaking toward me, yipping in delight at the momentous discovery that I was no longer sealed away in a closet but was now available to join in a game of tag.

Which was just what it must have seemed when I started running. Even before I heard Mike Vamp behind me, I was racing across the yard and around the corner of the porch. No wonder I hadn't been detected when I crept down the hall! No wonder the house had seemed so improbably quiet! I hadn't been heard, because there had been no one to hear me. Vamp had not been waiting for my parents in the living room; instead, he had been lying in wait for them in the yard.

At the end of the drive, Lorelei's car lights seemed to beckon to me. In my rush to reassure myself that the car in the ditch was unoccupied, I had neglected to turn off the headlights of the Porsche, and they now blazed forth like twin beacons in a low-set lighthouse. With those to guide me, I increased my speed as I ran, terribly conscious of the pounding footsteps behind me. I had in my favor the fact that I knew the terrain, the location of all the shrubbery, trees, and potholes. I easily skirted the bushes that lined the driveway and could tell by his curses that my pursuer had collided with them. Porky was still barking gleefully as he scampered along behind me, having a fine old time. Then I heard a yelp and a thud and another burst of swearing and realized that Vamp had stumbled over the dog, giving me a chance to increase the distance between us.

I reached the car, hurled myself into it, and slammed the door, punching the lock a split second before Vamp's hand struck the handle. I reached frantically down to see if the key was in the ignition. To my relief, it was, and I gave it a savage twist, rewarded by a guttural rumble of protest. I tried again, and this time was greeted by silence. Even to someone who knew as little about cars as I did, it was obvious that the lights had run down the battery.

The muzzle of a pistol was now pressed to the window.

"Unlock that door and get out of the car," Vamp shouted, his gentlemanly facade a thing of the past. "Your father's the one I want, not you or your grandmother. When my job here is done, the rest of the family can go."

He made it sound so inevitable—"when my job here is done"—as though my father's murder were a foregone conclusion. Staring out through the window into the face of death, I wondered if those strange eyes had ever held light, even when they belonged to a newborn baby. Jim had been right when he'd said happy endings weren't mandatory. This was no TV drama, it was hard-core reality. I had been the creator of this true-life drama, and I was the one responsible for its ending.

What I did next wasn't planned, it simply happened. Without shifting my gaze from Vamp's, I slid my right arm between the bucket seats and groped until my hand closed upon the handle of my tennis racket. Then I switched off the headlights, and the yard went black. The thin slip of moon was once again shrouded in clouds, and the lighted front window of the house was shielded by bushes.

With my left hand I picked up the flashlight, my thumb on the switch.

"You win," I said. "I'll get out," and I opened the door.

If I'd had more time to think, I might not have done it. I'd been raised by parents who never had lifted a hand to me, and my only exposure to violence had been from movies. To keep myself from panicking, I blocked out the present and pictured myself on a tennis court in the early morning with cocky, self-assured Larry standing across from me. "You're pretty good for a girl!" I heard him call tauntingly, and I willed myself to respond with exaggerated anger.

Sliding out of the car, I turned on the flashlight and directed the beam into the startled eyes of the hitman. The sudden, blinding glare caught him unawares, and I didn't pause to find out how he was going to react to it. With my right hand gripping the racket handle and my legs widespread for balance, I swung my serving arm up and over my head. I told myself the pale oval was a tennis ball and this was the serve that was going to decide the match. It seemed as though I was moving very slowly, but actually it all happened in a matter of seconds. With my arm stretched high in the air, I turned the racket on edge and brought it slicing down with all my strength directly into the face of the man in front of me.

The blow landed so hard that the racket flew out of my hand, and the hitman went staggering back to the edge of the ditch. For a moment he teetered there like a circus performer gone out of control on a highwire, spotlighted by the cruel white beam of the flashlight. Then his eyes rolled back and his legs crumbled under him, and as I stood there motionless, paralyzed with horror, he went plunging backward over the edge of the embankment.

The soul-chilling sound of the splash snapped me back into motion. With a few swift strides I was at the edge of the drainage ditch, staring down into what was now a fast-flowing river. The beam of the flashlight played across the surface, but there was no sign of either a man or a vampire. The hitman was gone, as though he had never existed.

And perhaps he hadn't, I thought. Had he ever been real? Perhaps he was just a figment of a fever dream. Perhaps I would wake in the morning in Princess April's Chamber and smile at the silly nightmare that had seemed so real to me. But even as I tried to make myself believe that, I was sliding down the embankment into the ditch, preparing to undertake the most gruesome search of my life.

I walked that portion of ditch at least three dozen times that night, feeling around with my feet for what I didn't want to find. When I was finally able to concede it was hopeless, I didn't have enough strength left to climb back out again. I don't know how long I stood there in water up to my rib cage, fighting the pull of the current and waiting for morning. It might have been hours, it might have been only minutes, but that was where it was that my family found me when Tom Geist drove the three of them home from the hospital.

It was my father who climbed into the ditch to get me, and carried me in his arms back up to the house. Tom remained to continue the search for the body, which he found wedged between the front wheels of the Plymouth and the culvert. Then, as the sky in the east began to grow light and the branches of the trees filled with riotous birdsong, we gathered in our living room to compose the final chapter of the Weber family story.

"You'll have to admit it's ironic," Lorelei said wryly. "We finally have something in common, and it has to be this."

"Our situations aren't comparable," said Mother. "You didn't bring your injury on yourself. When Larry told me Valerie wasn't at Kim's house, I was so upset I just had to rush right over there, even though I knew I shouldn't be driving."

They were seated side by side in dilapidated armchairs, weighed down by identical casts on their right arms. I was scrunched up on the sofa with my feet in my father's lap and a blanket wrapped around me, for despite the heat of the room I was shivering uncontrollably. Jason lay sprawled on the floor with his head on Porky's haunches, and Tom

Geist stood by the door, regarding us all as though he had seen enough of us to last him forever.

"I guess you realize your life here is over," he said. "Security's impossible now. Vamp may be dead, but the people who hired him are not. Professional killers are a dime a dozen. If one falls down on the job, they send in another."

"We can never go back then?" asked Mother. "Is that what you're saying? We're going to have to stay in hiding forever?"

"It doesn't have to be that way," said my father. "No one can really know what happened here last night. Vamp could have murdered me before he met his own death. If so, there wouldn't be any further reason to search for me. All you'd need is a death certificate with my name on it, and the rest of you could go home and take up your lives again."

"Go home without you!" exclaimed Mother. "This is no time for joking."

"It's one solution," said Dad. "I think you should consider it. You were right when you said we'll have to keep hiding forever. As long as they think I'm alive, they'll consider me a danger."

"Then we'll start a new life somewhere else," Mother said determinedly.

"You can't do that as part of the program," Tom told her. "Relocation is almost always a one-shot deal. I may be able to pull enough strings to get you new documentation, but you can't expect to be subsidized by the government."

"Uncle Max can help us," said Bram. "He and Dad are buddies. If he was to ask—"

"Don't hold your breath," said Lorelei. "Now that Max has no more need of your father, I doubt very much that we can count on him for anything."

"I hate to believe that, but maybe it's true," said Dad. "At any rate, Max has no access to government funding. We can't keep reaching back for props to hang on to. If we're going to make a fresh start, it will be on our own. There's no one left to depend on except ourselves."

"And each other," Mother said softly.

"Yes—and each other," said Dad. "Do you think that will be enough to build a new life with?"

At first I thought the question was directed at Mother, but then I saw that he meant it for me as well.

"Of course," Mother said immediately, but I remained silent. The truth was, I wasn't too sure that it *would* be enough for us. Still, what choice did we have? We had burned our bridges, and there was nothing left for us to do but move onward.

"Do you think we can do it?" Dad asked me. His eyes were hopeful, and I knew that he desperately wanted some reassurance.

Despite my reservations, I found myself nodding.

"This time I'm choosing my own name, though," I told him.

EPILOGUE

It was December when I first saw the boy at the shopping mall.

Of course, today I don't think of him as "the boy" anymore; he has a name and a place of his own in my life. At the time, though, that's all he was, just a teenage boy, standing by himself at a department store window, while crowds of holiday shoppers shoved their way past him.

December is a month that is rife with nostalgia. If there's anything deep in your heart that you want to keep buried, you can count on December to bring it to the surface. That's probably why I saw him, or at least why I noticed him. Maybe it was my way of putting the past December behind me, or maybe I had a longing to live it over again.

I had gone to the mall to take my brother Christmas shopping, since Mother works as a secretary for an insurance company and doesn't have the time to do that sort of thing anymore. Nor does my grandmother, who works at the Empress Boutique, a shop that specializes in high-fashion clothing. My father hasn't found a permanent job yet, but at Christmastime he was working at a sporting goods store. He said it felt strange to have come full circle and be selling skis as he did when he first met Mother.

I now have a job myself, my first one ever. I got it to earn some spending money for Christmas and then decided to keep it until I graduate. On weekends I work at Burger King. It's sort of fun, except for the awful uniform, but at least my hair's not long enough to need a hair net. It has grown out some, but it still doesn't reach my collar, and it's going to take a long time to get it like it used to be. I'm wondering now if it's worth the effort to grow it. It's easier to take care of when it's short like this.

I'd been playing it cautious, keeping to myself a lot, determined never again to get too close to anybody. Then I saw this boy—dark-haired and tall, wearing a red and white rugby shirt—and my breath went out of me in a painful gasp. He had his back turned toward me, and I moved forward until I was standing next to him at the window and saw that he was looking at a crystal prism.

I'm usually very wary about talking to strangers, but I couldn't stop myself this time. Without my ever intending it, I heard myself say to him, "I had one of those once, and it really meant a lot to me." Actually, I still had the prism in a dresser drawer. It had been in one of the boxes we'd brought back from Norwood.

He turned to face me, surprised, yet obviously pleased.

"Well, hi," he said. "I wouldn't have guessed you'd know me."

"Oh?" I hadn't the slightest idea who he was.

"I've been sitting across from you all semester in chemistry. Whenever you turn around, I try to make eye contact, but you look right through me like I was made out of glass."

"I'm sorry," I said. "It hasn't been intentional."

"I'm glad." He smiled, and a dimple appeared at one corner of his mouth. He wasn't as handsome as Steve, and now that I saw him straight on from the front, there was less resemblance than I'd thought. Still, he was attractive, no doubt about that. He had an open face with an easy grin, and clear, light eyes that were fringed with surprisingly long lashes.

"The prism's pretty," I said. "Are you considering it for your girlfriend?"

"For my mother," he said. "Do you think it's something a mother might go for? What do you do with it anyway, wear it on a chain?"

"You hang it in a window, so the sun shines through it," I said. "The prism fractures the light and throws out rainbows. It's supposed to be a symbol of new beginnings."

"That's a nice idea." He wasn't looking at the prism. "Like I said, I've been watching you in class, trying to think how to meet you. I figured you were new this year or, for sure, I'd know you."

"We moved here in September just before school started."

"Have you had a chance to get to know many of the kids yet?"

"It's not that easy when you enter a school in your senior year," I told him. "Especially when you're not into sports or anything."

"Would you like to go out sometime, and I'll introduce you around?" He was trying to sound casual, but his face had gone suddenly scarlet. There was something oddly endearing about his blushing. "With the holidays coming up, there are going to be parties."

My mind flew back to one party—one special party—and one special boy who danced with me in the firelight, his breath tinged with chocolate, a strand of silver in his hair. I clung to that precious memory, letting myself savor it, experiencing once again the flavor of first love. Then I shoved the memory out of my mind and sent it spinning down into the vast cavern of might-have-beens.

"That would be nice," I said. "I love Christmas parties."

That evening, when I got home, I hung up my prism.